A HALF-TAIL UPRISING

A HALF-TAIL UPRISING

A Sequel

BRETT WIREBAUGH

RESOURCE *Publications* · Eugene, Oregon

A HALF-TAIL UPRISING
A Sequel

Resource Publications
An Imprint of Wipf and Stock Publishers
199 W. 8th Ave., Suite 3
Eugene, OR 97401

www.wipfandstock.com

PAPERBACK ISBN: 978-1-5326-9004-4
HARDCOVER ISBN: 978-1-5326-9005-1
EBOOK ISBN: 978-1-5326-9006-8

Manufactured in the U.S.A.   11/19/20

Dedicated to Wilson, Payton, Gabe, and Abbie whose enthusiasm for the first book compelled me to write a sequel. By the way, see if you can find yourselves appearing in cameo roles somewhere in the book!

And to Meema, whose quiet strength and love remain the foundation of the Wirebaugh family.

"God undertook the most dramatic rescue operation in cosmic history.
He determined to save the human race from self-destruction, and
He sent His Son Jesus Christ to salvage and redeem them.
The work of man's redemption was accomplished at the cross."

—Billy Graham

"Then will the lame leap like a deer, and the mute tongue shout for joy.
Water will gush forth in the wilderness and streams in the desert."

—Isaiah 35:6 (NIV)

CONTENTS

PROLOGUE

"A last note from your narrator: I am haunted by humans."

—MARKUS ZUSAK IN *THE BOOK THIEF* (2005)

First came the boom that roared and echoed across the valley. The shrieks of birds and flapping of wings followed in unison out of nearby trees. Next came the howling of children. The disturbance was loud enough to spook not only the horses, but also the adolescent horseback riders. Two camp workers took charge and led the group quickly back to the welcome building. Down on the paintball course, the players were panic-stricken mid-game, first by the loud blast, then by a couple of peculiar masked gunmen who themselves violently erupted from the dense brush. Only theirs weren't paintball guns. Their appearance after the bang was clearly no coincidence—the explosion was their cue. The children and teachers were paraded at gunpoint back through the woods toward the front of the camp. It became clear as the entire seventh grade converged together that they were the victims of some kind of a coordinated attack. The thought ran through many of their heads—why would anybody want to hold an entire seventh grade hostage? They were driven to the back wall of the Welcome Center and forced to huddle together in whimpering clumps where they awaited instructions. They didn't have to wait long. The click and whine of a megaphone overpowered their muffled sobs. A male voice trumpeted through the fear. "STOP CRYING AND LISTEN TO ME NOW."

1

BLOOD

"Now listen, Doctor, and I'll tell you something.
Did you know that animals can talk?"

—HUGH LOFTING IN *DOCTOR DOOLITTLE* (1920)

FRIDAY

He had one job. As the bodyguard to the great Half-tail, the enormous blacktail buck's one job was to protect twelve-year-old Dolby. It was such a high honor from Fantasma the Wise—the albino doe—that he had remained in tiny Gomer, Michigan to commit himself to the boy's safety. In his words that only Dolby and other deer could understand, "Shadow Muzzle job—guard Half-tail. Shadow stay—watch for danger. Shadow like being Half-tail's shadow!" In Shadow Muzzle's defense, it was now early June and it had already been four months of peace since the big showdown. However, it was no longer called *Operation Deer Preserve* as it had been during the battle planning. It took just four short months for *Half-Tail Triumph* to become the new name fondly given by the nation's deer and elk population for their overwhelming victory spearheaded by Dolby. Half-Tail Triumph was the height of celebration for a generation of threatened deer. But even four months can lull one to sleep when there is not even a sniff of danger in the air. That is why Shadow let his guard down this day and lost sight of the hero—literally losing sight of him by falling asleep in the cool woods. The massive buck snorted awake to the nightmare of screams coming from the direction of Gomer Lake.

He was bald and short and scrawny, reminding one of a cartoon character. He even drove the campground golf cart like a cartoon. But the little golf buggy did share the garage with a restored, souped-up muscle car. The fire-engine red 1970 Chevrolet Chevelle SS 454 was as impressive as the golf cart was unimpressive. The sad little man never drove it anymore, but merely tinkered with it as a hobby. People who didn't know him assumed wrongly that the reason he owned a muscle car was to make up for his own lack of muscle. The man stumbled onto the cart which was labeled on the driver's side with the initials "P.V." After inserting the key, his foot stomped on the gas pedal. He looked behind him to pull out of the garage in reverse. The problem was that the machine was in drive! The golf cart lurched forward, jerking the man's unexpecting neck backwards, and slammed into a workbench of tools. After the echo of clanging metal subsided, the campground manager dropped his head onto the steering wheel. His voice echoed through the shed. "I'll bet Veep has never done that." Angry at himself and with life, he grabbed the closest thing within reach and hurled a pipe wrench at nothing in particular. With a sigh, the strange little man clicked the lever into reverse, the vehicle beeped repeatedly, and he backed out into freedom.

Four hundred pounds of muscle charged toward the lake. The crashing through the woods would have sounded to anyone within earshot like a Sherman tank mowing down trees at forty-five miles per hour. That same observer probably would have also found it funny to see the great beast slow down and try to silently sneak up to where the trees opened to the water. Shadow's antlers rose. His ears rotated in the air like a submarine periscope hunting for enemies. His wet, black nose searched the air for clues. The animal's eyes squinted with alarm as loud slaps and thuds welcomed him to the clearing. A low growl escaped his throat at the realization that the smell wafting into his nostrils was the unmistakable scent of his friend and responsibility—Dolby Hart.

For people that didn't know him, it was hard to believe that he wasn't older than his fifty-eight years. Percy looked like he was easily in his seventies, and frankly, acted like an ornery, old man. It was also hard to believe the age of his twin brother Perry, whose Hollywood good-looks and build made him seem never to have left his thirties. As the manager of Gomer's only campground, Percy's job was to keep it from getting any more run-down than it already was. Every day he toured the park with tools on-hand to fix the endless needs of the place. But, where to start? With so many problems, it could get overwhelming. So, he never actually got around to fixing much. As he kicked up dust and raced down the gravel road, he laughed to himself—if he could only fix his brother!

Shadow burst though the cover of the pine trees in time to see what looked like a crime scene. Dolby and his friend Steele Canis stood like statues with panicked looks on their marble faces. The boys were covered from head to toe in dark blood and some kind of thick muck. When the startled friends realized it was their protector who had interrupted them, they began the laughter of the relieved. Confused, Shadow Muzzle bellowed, "Shadow hear screaming. Shadow see blood. Half-tail okay?" Steele heard the grunts, but of course, didn't understand the meaning since he was merely human and not among those who understood animals. Dolby, quite possibly the only half-tail alive that could communicate with deer, came to his rescue.

With a cheesy grin and two thumbs confidently pointing at his own chubby chest, he bragged, "He is asking if the Half-tail is all right."

Steele playfully took offense and raised his arms in protest. "Hey! What about the no-tail?" He pointed back-and-forth at himself and their friend Adele Brown, who sat on the shore with her dog Zeke. "Weren't you worried about us no-tails?"

After a few wheezes of interpretation from Dolby, Shadow Muzzle sneezed a snort, ignoring the fifteen-year-old's questions. A large hoof stamped the ground as he impatiently and loudly demanded, "Why Half-tail bloody?"

Dolby looked down at his once-white shirt and gagged. Upon closer examination, Shadow Muzzle noticed what looked and smelled like animal guts mixed with the red streaks. Adele, despite being quiet and shy, wanted in on the discussion. Sensing the animal's question, she yelled with the disgust of a mother, "According to Steele, they were frog-gigging."

Dolby explained in deer tongue. "Not *exactly* frog-giggin'. We didn't have any spears, so we just used these baseball bats." Shadow's muzzle twisted sideways the way a dog's does when it seems confused. "We were seeing who could kill the most frogs . . . like this one." Dolby excitedly picked up a fresh kill by its bloody leg and tossed it in Adele's general direction. Adele screamed what was now a familiar scream to Shadow. He shook his head side-to-side with annoyance. The stag made a mental note to watch Dolby more closely.

Steele laughed and yelled, "I thought you were a tomboy?!" Farmer Brown's daughter immediately responded, but not verbally, as a mutilated frog carcass smacked Steele across the face.

2

FROGS

"After Moses and Aaron left Pharaoh,
Moses cried out to the LORD about the frogs . . .
And the LORD did what Moses asked. The frogs died in the houses,
in the courtyards, and in the fields."

—Exodus 8:12–13

SPLAT! Dolby's Louisville Slugger aluminum weapon stuck in the murky mud. "Strike one, Dough-boy!" yelled Steele from across the lake. SPLAT! "Strike two!" he laughed.

"Just worry about yourself," came the echoed retort.

Two more SPLATS answered Dolby—one from a bat striking an unsuspecting bullfrog, and the other from the sound of the dead amphibian smacking the water after a short toss by the boy. "That's number seventeen for me!" sang Steele as a fish crashed through the surface to enjoy an afternoon snack.

"You guys are gross," Adele shouted. "Are you done trying to show off?"

"Trying? Who's trying? I've fed the fish seventeen times. How many have you killed, Dough-boy?"

"I don't remember," came the embarrassed reply. He remembered.

Adele helped jog his memory. "I remember, Dolby—it's six. So, that makes the score Steele seventeen, Dolby six." She was enjoying getting him back for tossing the frog at her earlier. "Seventeen to six. Wow—so that means he's more than doubled your score!"

"I can do math, Adele."

"Actually, it's almost three times what you've done." Adele was enjoying herself a little too much, thought Dolby. At that moment, he discovered an old tennis ball stuck in the mud. Prying it loose, he looked at Zeke, Adele's Golden Lab, who seemed bored laying by her side. Though not much of an athlete, Dolby reached back and tossed the ball right up to the shore where Adele was lounging. Water sprayed at Adele, but that wasn't what Dolby was ultimately hoping for. Zeke—man's best friend—came through. The dog bounded into the water, doggy-paddled toward the floating prize, scooped up the ball in his mouth, and dutifully returned it to Adele for another throw.

"Wait for it!" Dolby yelled to whoever would listen.

"AAAAAAAHHH!!" Zeke had dropped the ball in Adele's lap and then proceeded to violently twist side-to-side to drench her with a shower of dirty lake water. Steele and Dolby's laughter were interrupted by another shout, this time from a golf cart that had slithered up to the lake.

"What are you brats doing?" Percy looked as nervous and sweaty as ever.

"Um, just skipping rocks, Pee Wee," replied Steele. The boys each made a sidearm throw to demonstrate.

Percy's blood boiled hotter. "You know not to call me that, Steele." Steele knew his nickname but actually hadn't meant to use it. The golf cart inched closer making everyone even more uncomfortable. Fortunately, a young couple arrived on the scene at that moment. They peddled by on brand new mountain bikes, laughing and making eyes at each other as if they were newlyweds. Their interruption stopped Percy from getting any closer. "I have my eyes on you both," he said ironically. He was actually looking around. "You are just lucky that Miss Brown was here. I trust *her*." Adele smiled way too wide in the boys' direction. "Just watch yourselves and don't forget . . ."

"Yes, sir?" snapped Dolby.

"I will be watching you."

"Yessir," came the chorus of three voices. Percy peeled away in his cart as if to add emphasis to whatever little fear he could instill.

"What a loser," summarized the soon-to-be high schooler.

"But, see what I mean? You heard him . . . 'I will be watching you.' I'm telling you something is coming. I can feel it."

"This again, Dolby?" sighed Adele. "Your paranoia is driving us crazy. Nobody is out to get you or the deer anymore. Edith and Cliff Krantz are safely behind bars for trying to destroy you and all the deer."

"Yeah, and they are so ancient, there's no way they will ever see the light of day again. You have nothing to be afraid of," added Steele.

"But what if they had helpers—accomplices—that haven't been caught yet? They could right now be hatching some kind of plan to do me in." Dolby heard the words come out of his mouth, and even he had to admit to himself that he sounded a little crazy. But was he? They didn't understand the pressure on him being the only half-tail friend of whitetail deer.

"You mean like the lunch lady? Or Mildred the librarian? Or Jed Calhoun? Or Chief Kowalski?" Adele listed just a few of the so-called suspects that Dolby had mentioned in the past four months. "I'm starting to think you just *want* something to happen so that you can be a hero again, instead of just being a regular middle school kid." Adele was making a lot of sense. Dolby hated that she always made a lot of sense. He did miss being the great Half-tail. He missed it a lot. She was getting too personal. Time to change the subject.

"Hey! What's the deal with that guy? Why do some people call him *Pee Wee*, or *Peev*, and others use *P.V.*?"

Adele chimed in. "I've also heard him referred to as *Peevy.*"

Steele knew. Adele knew a lot of stuff, but this kind of thing was Steele's specialty. He laughed. "His name is Percy and his last name starts with a V. I guess it's a long, hard-to-pronounce last name, so people shortened it to *Percy V.*, then *P.V.*, which turned into *Peev*. Of course, behind his back, he's *Pee Wee*. It's been so long I don't remember if I ever really knew his last name in the first place."

"So, Veep is his brother, right?"

"Yep, it's his twin brother, the one who owns most of Gomer—the movie theater, post office, hardware store, Marino's Pizza, and even Hideaway Campground—extremely successful dude."

"Which is why Peev even has a job."

"Probably. Veep also owns and runs Gomer Ranch where we grew up going to summer camp." Steele knew that Dolby, being new to Gomer, had never experienced the tradition that was summer camp at the ranch.

"Everybody knows that!" Adele fondly remembered all the fun she had with Uncle Veep all those summers ago. All the kids called him Uncle Veep. "What is Uncle Veep's actual name, then?"

His name is Perry—*Perry V.*, which became *P.V.*, a nickname that was confusing because of his brother. So, somehow the initials were reversed and *V.P.* or *Veep* won out." Satisfied with Steele's explanation, the three youngsters sat quietly and looked out over the shimmering water. It was a serene moment until . . . SPLAT!

"Got 'em!" Steele's baseball bat landed a successful blow. Blood and guts splattered the friends.

"UGH! STEELE!" Adele wiped goo from her eyes.

Dolby did the same but couldn't help thinking that he could possibly be the next victim to go *SPLAT.*

3

THUNDERSTICK

"You take a guy like Morrow that's always snapping their towel at people's
(backsides)—really trying to *hurt* somebody with it—they don't just stay
a rat while they're a kid. They stay a rat their whole life."

—J.D. SALINGER IN *CATCHER IN THE RYE* (1951)

Three kids and a dog took one last plunge into the water to rinse off as
much frog filth as possible. They knew it was either wash off in dirty
Gomer Lake or use the gross campground showers, which was like being given the choice between going hungry and eating Geema's Liver and
Onions. The foul smell and slimy texture grew to be too much for Adele. "I
will NEVER eat Frog Legs again!"

"Wait? You've eaten Frog Legs before?" asked an impressed Dolby.

"No, but I *promise* I never will now."

"Hey Adele?" Steele got Dolby's attention and gave him a *watch this*
look. She glared his way. "Did you know that's not just frog guts that are
smeared all over you?" The glare got more intense. "You are also probably
covered in frog poop!"

She hadn't thought of that. "Awwww . . . I HATE YOUR GUTS!" She
heard the words that just escaped her lips, looked down at her arms, and
muttered, "I HATE MY GUTS, TOO," referring to the frog remnants still
remaining on her skin. She gingerly flicked a string of frog goo onto the
ground.

The three friends made an unlikely trio walking the dusty road back to Hideaway Campground. The oldest was tall, muscular, confident, and in need of a shave despite just finishing the eighth grade. The other boy—still small for his age; still sporting red hair and freckles; still remaining on the chubby side—waddled along as if he didn't really belong anywhere. To look at him, you would have never believed he could've been the Half-tail hero of Operation Deer Preserve. Adele, taller than Dolby but far shorter than Steele, looked every bit the part of the stereotypical farmer's daughter—plain, unassuming, capable. School had just let out for the summer, and they always looked forward to the traditional Memorial Day weekend at the campground. That is, they looked forward to everything except . . .

"NOOOOOO!" Dolby was the first to hear the sound. "Already? It's Friday and not even four o'clock yet."

Steele shook his head and spit at the dirt. "Gets worse and worse every year."

"And so, it begins," sighed Adele. Off in the distance, four overly ex-cited grandpas sang together in four-part harmony without the aid of an instrument. It was the first of many barbershop quartets to descend upon Gomer's campground over the course of the next four days for what posters and websites called "The International Barbershop Quartet Competition."

"You know they call it an *international* barbershop contest?" Steele said, his words dripping with sarcasm. "I guess by *international* (he raised his hands and fingers to make air quotes) they mean groups coming all the way from Waynesville and Fleming's Mill. Dolby and Adele both laughed while also wanting to cry. They walked in silence preparing their minds for waking up to *Let me Call you Sweetheart*, sitting around the fire while dozens of quartets crooned at the same time, and falling asleep to *Shine On, Harvest Moon*. They shuffled on toward the music as if they were death row convicts being dragged to the electric chair.

"Down by the Old Mill Stream." Dolby's voice broke the silence.

"What's that Dough-boy?"

"*Down by the Old Mill Stream*—that's what they're singing." He hated that he knew that, but this wasn't his first barbershop rodeo. Dolby and his Mom made it a priority to visit Geema every year over Memorial Day for the sole purpose of joining her on this camping trip. It meant a lot to Geema because they knew she enjoyed the morning-'til-evening acapella singing more than the rest of her family. For the first time, the title *Down by the Old Mill Stream* meant something to Dolby. It was just around 120 days ago that he almost died at the old Gomer Grist Mill. His mind flew back to the moment when he was carried in the air by Mortimer Moose's broad, flat antlers in a victory parade of deer, elk, caribou, and human friends that rivaled the tickertape parade of any championship sports team. But, all of a sudden, right in the middle of his trip down glory days lane, an explosion of noise in the woods to his right threatened to turn the daydream into a nightmare. The teens stopped in their tracks. Dolby's mind now raced to the worst-case scenario. There *was* someone out to get him. All three listened, but the noise had stopped. They looked at each other. They looked behind them. They looked around. The sounds of old-timey music in the distance only made the waiting more eerie. After a couple of minutes, they slowly began their trek again, but this time with ears wide open. CRACK! There it was again! Steele grabbed a walking stick and began waving it around toward an invisible attacker.

"OUCH!" The boys jerked around to see Adele rubbing the back of her head. "Something hit me!"

"OW! Me too!" Steele picked up the missile that was rolling in the dust. "An acorn?"

Dolby's heart started pumping again. "Are you serious? SNOWFLAKE?!"

On many occasions, Dolby's pet, and oldest deer friend, would spit acorns at him just because. Snowflake leaped out of the cover and hopped around the group clearly exulting in her prank. Although only eleven-months-old, the fawn looked bigger to Dolby than he'd remembered—possibly even full grown.

"Igotchaagain, didn't I, Dolbyoldboy? Youshoulddaseenthelookon-yourface! Thatwasawesome! Gotchagotchagotchagotcha . . ." Dolby tried but couldn't stay mad at his good friend and promptly wrestled her to the ground.

After the dust settled, the four headed back to camp. Dolby's mind raced with concern and took advantage of some one-on-one time with Snowflake. "Can I ask you a question?"

"Sure, but only on one condition."

"What's that?"

"I get to hang out with your family at the campsite tonight."

Dolby wished he could honor her request. "You know we can't do that. What are people going to think with a 100-pound deer just sitting around with humans? Besides, I am trying to conceal my Half-tail identity. Have you heard, or seen, or smelled anything fishy lately?"

"Only by the lake—get it?!"

"You know what I mean!"

"No. Nothing is happening that I can tell. What makes you so jumpy?"

"Nothing . . . everything. I don't know. Just got a feeling."

"Well, I can tell you for sure that there has been no influx of visiting moose, elk, deer, or caribou to the Gomer area, so we are fine. There has been no Fantasma sighting, and no activity at Base Camp. Boy, that whole thing earlier in the year has really got you spooked."

"Maybe you're right." Dolby lied. Why wouldn't anybody listen to him? He wanted to scream at everybody, "Hey! I'm the freakin' Half-tail. And guess what? You're not. I know what I'm talking about." But he didn't yell. Instead he asked another question. "What do you know about that creepy Peev guy who takes care of the campground?"

"Not much, except . . ."

"Except what?"

"I do have it on good authority that he likes to use the thunderstick." Dolby had learned early on that a thunderstick was deer-speak for a hunting rifle. "I mean, he *really* likes to use the thunderstick." Lots of people in Gomer hunted for sport—this was mid-Michigan after all. Even school was canceled on the first day of every hunting season. But, something about Snowflake's comments about Peev gave Dolby pause. He suddenly pictured a smiling Peev holding a Model 70 Winchester hunting rifle as big as he was and stating mechanically, "I'll be watching you."

"Snowflake?"

"Yes?"

"Could you do me a favor and not tell anyone about ole' Peevy? I think he is up to no good. I've got to figure out what to do, but no one will believe me."

"Dolby?"

"Yes?"

"You know I can't actually tell anyone? Your friends don't speak whitetail."

"Right. Good point."

4

HOBO

"Perhaps the greatest charm of tramp-life is the absence of monotony.
In Hobo Land . . . the impossible happens and the unexpected jumps out of the
bushes at every turn of the road. The hobo never knows what is going to happen
the next moment; hence, he lives only in the present moment."

—JACK LONDON IN *THE ROAD* (1907)

Steele and Adele went left as Snowflake and Dolby went right. "See, I *am* heading in the right direction," he chuckled to himself. The families of his two no-tail friends were also spending Memorial Day at the campground. They promised to meet up that night or the next morning.

Snowflake made one last push, "Let me stay with you at the camp!"

"All right, fine. I'll ask." The doe hid herself in the bushes just outside of Dolby's two-man tent hoping for a positive response. Snowflake knew that it was a Friday night tradition for the Hart's to make campfire Hobo dinner, and that Geema would fix her a special tin foil packet filled with carrots, potatoes, and onions.

"Geema?"

The gray-haired matriarch of the family didn't even look up from her chopping board. "The answer is no," she said with a smile.

Dolby was used to her kidding. "Can Snowflake join us for dinner? She really misses you." Dolby often laid it on thick, but not too thick, to get what he wanted. She may have been old, but she was extremely wise. It was true, however, that Snowflake had outgrown living at their house and missed seeing Geema every day.

"You know we can't risk that, deary." It was a topic discussed so often that Geema didn't even bother giving a reason.

"Aw, come on. Kit gets to hang out with Mom." Kit was a fox that they had raised since it was a pup. As a Half-tail to the fox species, Karen Withers-Hart had played a major role in Dolby's big victory back in February.

"Son, you know Kit was injured and needs to be nursed back to health," Karen said.

Dolby never used to stand up to his Mom. "So, that was four months ago. Pretty sure he is fine now."

Karen smirked proudly as if to say at the same time, "Good point," and, "that's my boy." Karen shot a look at her mother. "Okay, Dolby. But she has to wait until after sunset."

"Thanks Mom!" Dolby said with a kiss on her cheek.

A quartet in a campsite right next to them began a rendition of *Sweet Adeline* which caused Geema to drop her knife. "Oh, honey," she said aloud to her daughter. "This reminds me of your father. We used to dance to this at the VFW. It was at the VFW where we first started holding hands in our own special way, and the first place he called me his favorite." Geema missed her husband every day. "I love you more," she sighed to herself. Her trip down memory lane didn't last long. She was rudely interrupted by a grandson who could not care less.

"Humph." Dolby uttered a verbal sound of annoyance.

"Is there something you'd like to say, young man?" She knew that there was. Geema would have to visit memories of her husband at a later time.

"No. Yes. It's just . . . can't we ever go camping on a different weekend?"

Geema didn't answer, but her knife did. The cutting and slicing grew faster and more intense. Even his Mom's glare felt like a knife.

"I'm sorry, Geema. I'm just . . . you know . . . not a fan."

Geema was not so out-of-touch that she didn't understand that her style of music wasn't for everyone, especially a twelve-year-old boy. "I get it, Dolby. But you may be surprised to find that there are things that can be learned even from this style of music."

Dolby was trying to be respectful but couldn't help rolling his eyes about that one. "Yes, Geema." She also was discerning enough to know that at that moment, Dolby was not teachable.

With tongs, Karen removed the tin foil packets from the red, campfire coal. He heard a quartet start in on a barbershop standby called *Driving Me Crazy*. Dolby chuckled to himself. It had been a couple of hours later, so Dolby thought it was safe. He waited for Geema to put two and two together. When she did, she caught his eye. Dolby lip-synced along with the title words. Geema pointed a bony finger in his direction. "Don't start with me young man." She couldn't stop a giggle from escaping.

"Too soon?" he asked.

"Next year will be too soon!"

"I love you, Geema," he sang.

They prepared their plates and plopped down on camp chairs around the glowing embers. His mom gave Dolby another of her famous glares as Dolby tried unsuccessfully to quietly open the tin foil pouch on his plate. Geema was in the middle of saying grace. He knew better, but he still could not bring himself to close his eyes during prayer. It wasn't that he didn't believe—he had seen too much of the work of him who his deer friends called *The Windmaster* not to believe. He just had a hard time fully trusting— God or anybody. It was understandable, he thought, given that his Dad had left him at a young age, his Mom left during the worst of the attack on Gomer's deer population, his grandfather had passed away when he was young, and he had lived a lifetime of being the target of every bully ever. As he scalded his tongue on the first bite of steaming hamburger meat, the irony didn't escape him that he just continues to get burned. The idea at that moment of venturing out on his own without anyone's help had a certain appeal. "I could totally live free like a homeless person," he foolishly thought. Dolby looked up in time to see Snowflake emerge from the brush, and with a quick motion of his hand, tried to shoo the fawn back into hiding. Dolby cleared his throat in an attempt to hide a deer grunt. With a mouth full of potatoes and onions, he mumbled, "I told you I'd bring you your Hobo dinner at sunset." Snowflake ignored Dolby. The deer remained motionless at some faint commotion coming down the campground lane. Dolby and his mother and grandmother suddenly caught wind of a muffled voice coming through an amplified speaker.

5

PARADE

"I had a school . . . the privilege of living with youth, of helping to mould those young minds and of impressing them with one's own character and ideals, was very dear to me."

—SIR ARTHUR CONAN DOYLE
IN *HOUND OF THE BASKERVILLES* (1902)

Dolby, Karen, and Geema walked up to the campground's main drag to see, as Geema put it, what all the hubbub was about. Because so many other families staying at the campground had the same idea, the lined street gave the feeling that Gomer's annual Memorial Day parade had come early. Technically, it *was* a parade, just without the bands and floats. Leading the train were a dozen school-aged kids riding their bikes in the middle of the gravel road. Behind them traveling at about ten miles per hour was a black Dodge Ram pickup truck with the words *Gomer Ranch Ranger* painted on the side. More children trailed the vehicle—all hoping to catch up in order to climb the tailgate and into the bed. As the scene approached the Hart family, they began to both hear what was being said into the microphone, and who was saying it. "Dee? Has anybody seen Dee Earl? He has dark hair, eight-years-old, and was last seen by the camp store."

Karen turned to Dolby. "Isn't that the boy that got lost last year?" Dolby nodded and chuckled.

"He was last seen wearing a Central Michigan Chippewa sweatshirt," came the update, followed by a click.

"Of course!" cried Geema.

"Of course, what?" replied her daughter.

"Look who's driving."

With one hand on the wheel, and one on the handheld microphone, Perry V. himself was leading the rescue effort. He was proceeding slow enough that at times no hands were on the wheel as he waved to people in the crowd. He was the main attraction and honorary parade marshal of this procession. For many of the women of Gomer, he was the main attraction for a different reason.

Karen asked what many people were thinking. "Why is such a busy man spending his Friday night at a dumpy campground looking for a lost boy?"

"Remember it's *his* dumpy campground. Of all the businesses that he owns, it is clear to most'a the folks in Gomer—that man's heart is with the children of this town. That's why he spends so much more time at Gomer Ranch and the campground than anywhere else."

"How does he have time for his wife and stepson?" Karen wondered aloud.

"Well, my dear, I'm afraid he doesn't. A man like that's got too many balls in the air to juggle a home life too. But I reckon his wife don't care too much. She's livin' large in that big log cabin back'a'the woods by Gomer Ranch. Typical gold-digger situation if you ask me. Appears to me they got this convenient arrangement down pat—she uses his gold to become a good trophy wife. And look how the rug rats love him!" Sweaty kids lined up beside the driver's window just for a high-five. The truck continued to travel at a safe pace until the driver pulled up alongside Geema, Karen, and Dolby.

"Hello Miss Karen. Lookin' as beautiful as ever." Karen blushed. Veep then turned his attention toward Geema. "Well, now, who is this young lady? Karen, you didn't tell me you had a sister?! Wait, is that Edith With-ers? Shoot girl, you get younger every time I see you!"

Geema gushed. "Perry as I live and breathe!" Both of the ladies were red-cheeked now. Dolby knew Uncle Veep long enough to know that this wasn't just a show—he was ever the charmer.

"There he is—how's 'ole Dolby these days?" Nobody really knew how he remembered everyone's name.

"Fine, sir."

"You know to call me Uncle Veep! When you say sir, I look around for an Army general. You've got a birthday coming up, huh? The big one-three—thirteen years old! Teenage-life, here you come!"

Dolby almost blushed. Uncle Veep had a way of making one feel like he was the only person in the world that mattered. He also had a way of treating children and teens like they were as important, maybe even more important, than adults. "So, Dolby," Uncle Veep's tone turned suddenly serious. "It's starting to get dark. If we don't end up finding Dee in the next hour or so, would you and your friends be willing to help us continue the search?"

Dolby was shocked to be asked. "Maybe. Except I don't know if Steele or Adele are able."

"I wasn't talking about them. I wondered if you could enlist your *other* friends to help?" He punctuated the sentence with a sly wink. Dolby froze. Was he referring to his four-footed friends? How did he know about them? "You don't have to answer now," he said with a satisfied smile. "We'll talk later. Gotta go!" The truck inched away now with even more kids falling over each other in the flatbed.

"Man, that guy's like the mayor of this town," admired Karen.

Geema answered, "No, he's more mayor than our actual mayor is."

"Good point."

Dolby added, "He's also more campground manager than . . ." He was interrupted.

". . . than the actual campground manager?" Dolby's high from the conversation with Uncle Veep was instantly shattered. During the chaos, Veep's brother Peev had crept up in his golf cart right behind the Hart's. Dolby was sure he heard Peev mutter, "I hate kids," under his breath. He was also sure that he was looking straight at him when he said it. "Don't worry—I'm used to it. I can't compare to Mr. VIP himself. You're right, everything he touches turns to success. He's always doing good things for people; always building things for the community; always making everyone feel so good about themselves; always rescuing kids that are lost . . . blah, blah, blah." His tone dripped with bitterness.

This made Karen defensive. "What exactly is wrong with all of those things?"

Peev paused. "You don't see it do you? Nothing is wrong with doing those things, *unless* you are doing them at the expense of your family."

In the quiet of his tent, Dolby kept thinking about the interaction with Peev. He was thankful that a nearby quartet finally called it a night. They finished with an old standard called, *Hello Ma Baby*. It was a song that Dolby remembered mostly from an old Bugs Bunny cartoon that he used to watch with Geema. In that cartoon, it was performed by a singing frog whose owner was trying to get him into show business. As they wrapped it up, Dolby laughed that the frogs were after him for earlier. His chuckling ended as the song ended because a chorus of frogs began to out sing the few other barbershop quartets still going. They kept him awake as if they really were exacting revenge for their frog buddies from the lake. Or were they the very same frogs returned to haunt their murderer? Dolby nervously laughed off that thought and concluded that he must really be tired. As a way of calming his nerves, he traced the outline of the emergency deer whistle on the string around his neck. He decided to add a journal entry to the notebook that he also brought most places. It was time to start recording who was suspicious and why.

In order to hide the list as much as possible, Dolby opened the notebook to a random page in the middle of the journal where he could bury the sensitive information. He started by listing names. Dolby couldn't bring himself to include Veep on the list. At the time, it seemed far more reasonable that Dolby had just misunderstood Veep's comments than to suspect his involvement in any kind of an evil plot.

Suspects	Reasons for suspicions	Possible motives
1. Enid Schwartz—lunch lady		
2. Mildred Snodgrass—librarian		
3. Jed Calhoun—Turkey-town Owner		
4. Chief Kowalski—police chief		
5. Percy V. (Peev)—campground manager		
6. Bones—night watchman		
7. Miss Daken—6th grade teacher		

Next, Dolby brainstormed reasons why they appear in his list:

Suspects	Reasons for suspicions	Possible motive
1. Enid Schwartz—lunch lady	—always rude 2 me — serves food so bad could be poison	
2. Mildred Snodgrass—librarian	—rude 2 me	
3. Jed Calhoun—Turkey-town Owner	—big deer hunter	
4. Chief Kowalski—police chief	—rude 2 me —reputation 4 being corrupt	
5. Percy V. (Peev)—camp-ground manager	—rude 2 me —creepy, big hunter	
6. Bones—night watchman	—rude 2 me —creepy	
7. Miss Daken—6th grade teacher	—nobody is that nice	

The notebook laid in his lap for over ten minutes before he could come up with just one possible motive. He wrote it down and knew that more reasons were sure to come.

Suspects	Reasons for suspicions	Possible motive
1. Enid Schwartz—lunch lady	—always rude 2 me —serves food so bad could be poison	—???
2. Mildred Snodgrass—librarian	—rude 2 me	—???
3. Jed Calhoun—Turkey-town Owner	—big deer hunter	—suspects Steele involved in the killing of his turkeys
4. Chief Kowalski—police chief	—rude 2 me —reputation 4 being corrupt	—???
5. Percy V. (Peev)—campground manager	—rude 2 me —creepy, big hunter	—???
6. Bones—night watchman	—rude 2 me —creepy	—???
7. Miss Daken—6th grade teacher	—nobody is that nice	—???

6

DARKNESS

"My sleep wasn't peaceful, though. I have the sense of emerging
from a world of dark, haunted places where I traveled alone."

—SUZANNE COLLINS IN *MOCKINGJAY* (2010)

Dolby reclined on the oversized bean bag in his new treehouse elbow-deep in a bag of expired Wavy Lay's potato chips. He basked in the freedom of doing what he wanted when at Hart Castle because he knew Geema would never let him eat greasy snacks anywhere but at the kitchen table. He almost didn't notice due to the loud crunching. But out of nowhere, the night sounds of tree frogs, crickets, and katydids completely stopped—his first clue that something was wrong. He bolted from the beanbag in search of his trusty deer whistle. Where was it? Where did he leave it? It was last found around his neck on a necklace. It wasn't there. He felt like the room was spinning. Roundandroundandroundandround until OOOOF! Dolby lost his balance and landed in the middle of the tree fort. At that moment a silhouette of a head rose slowly in the north-facing opening of the fort. From the grinning mouth of Peev himself came the words, "I will be watching you!"

Dolby lurched back away from the window. Another face appeared in the window directly behind him. "I will be watching you!" screeched Mildred Snodgrass waving a book.

Starting to panic, Dolby had nowhere to go because to his right, Chief Kowalski appeared. "I will be watching you!"

Now from his left came the lunch lady— "I will be watching you!"

One after another, a new suspicious face forced its way on the scene chanting the same refrain. He recognized Veep, Jed Calhoun, Bones the campground's night watchman, and even teacher Miss Daken. Finally, they all morphed together into the bony face of Edith Krantz, the wolf half-tail who Dolby had defeated along with all of her Pitcoywolves. The next thing Dolby remembered was the sound of his own gasp and sitting upright in his sleeping bag with sweat dripping down his face. He grabbed the first thing he could find in the pitch dark to towel off. Before he realized it, he was wiping his forehead with a sock and a pair of underwear, both of which unfortunately had already been used. A deep breath calmed his tense muscles. He was both relieved that it was only a dream and troubled by the amount of anxiety that it revealed. Dolby was also surprised and bothered by the appearance of Veep in his nightmare. Is it possible that his subconscious brain knew something that his heart wouldn't let him believe about his beloved Uncle Veep? Should Veep now be added to his list of suspects?

The nightmare worked on Dolby like an energy drink. It was two hours later—three o'clock in the morning to be exact—and Dolby's eyes continued to stare with sleeplessness up at the ceiling of the tent. He was wrong to think that eating the rest of a bag of chili-cheese Fritos would help him fall asleep. He was hoping the stomach ache was due to eating too much and not because of the expiration date. Sometimes having secret knowledge of where to get expired snacks at a Frito-Lay distributor's dumpster was a curse. Throwing away the empty bag was just an excuse to do something other than lay there. Dolby ventured out into the quiet night and headed toward the closest trash barrel. Due to being foggy with fatigue, he didn't think much of the trash bin's lid lying on the ground. As he went to throw away the crumpled trash, he was startled by a fat raccoon who himself was startled by Dolby's approach. "AAAH! Stupid trash panda!" Without thinking, Dolby had used another of Steele's funny nicknames. Steele was known to call skunks *fart kittens* and crawfish *mudbugs*. At one time, he even called deer *forest rats* but stopped once he found out about Dolby's abilities. As he watched the scavenger scurry away with his ringed-tail bobbing behind him, two other raccoons joined the escape. As they disappeared, Dolby saw glowing dots look back at him in the darkness. He noted that they really did look like masked bandits who were up to no good. Once again, he laughed to himself at the phrase *trash panda*, when he was suddenly blinded by a beam of light.

In different campsites, Adele and Steele were also wide awake, but for different reasons. The boys promised Adele that on Saturday morning they would do what she wanted since it was their choice to hit home runs with toads that day. They agreed to go back to the lake, but this time to do some fishing. Adele loved to fish, but truth be told, she never slept much on these camping trips regardless of what was on the agenda. Steele laid awake roasting in a tattered sleeping bag. He was alone in his tent awaiting the return of his father, who was hopefully just working late at the old motel. It had been a number of years since Swampy Canis, long considered the town drunk, had taken a sip. But that didn't erase the memories of the times Swampy had come home looking to take out his anger on anyone who happened to be in the way. He didn't realize it yet, but he had been trained over the years by his father to keep one eye open, especially late at night. He also hadn't realized yet that his own tendency to bully others was a pre-emptive strike to hurt others before they had the opportunity to hurt him first.

"Somm'in funny?" Dolby shielded the flashlight glare with his hands. "What'choo doin' out this time'a night? Nuttin' good happens after midnight—ain't'cho' momma never told yoo dat?"

"No, but my Geema tells me that all the time."

"Well, I'm gone tell tha' Grammaw of yours if'n you don' hightail it back to her."

"Yessir."

It didn't seem to Dolby that Bones knew who he was. Everybody knew him though—he was the only campground night watchman that anyone could remember. In fact, he lives in a one-room apartment above the maintenance garage, so he was always around. Skinny as a rail and pale as a ghost, he had frightened Dolby tonight as if he were an actual phantom. Nobody really knew if his nickname came from being so thin, or from working the graveyard shift, or both. Bones was halfway through a Slim Jim and used it as a pointer to jog Dolby's memory about where he was supposed to be. If Dolby hadn't been so scared, he would have found it comical that the Slim Jim of people was eating the Slim Jim of snacks. "Go on . . . git." He looked tired with dark circles under his eyes. Dolby figured that working third shift would do that to a guy.

"Mr. Bones, sir?" Dolby squeaked. "Can't something be done to get rid of all these raccoons? The place is infested with them." Bones wearily chewed the meat stick and muttered, "Naw. Mister Peevs likes 'em around for eating up insects-n-rats-n-snakes-n-garbage and whatnot. But I reckon I shouldn'a tole y'all that, huh?"

7

NOD

"'Rat race is a perfect name for it," she said. "We're always going and going and going, and never asking where. Did you ever hear of having more than you wanted? So that you couldn't want anything else and then started looking for something else to want? It seems like we're always searching for something to satisfy us, and never finding it."

—S.E. Hinton in *The Outsiders* (1967)

SATURDAY

Dolby woke up having to squint due to the brightness of the sun. He had overslept. "What time is it?" came the muffled yell through the t-shirt he was wrestling over his head.

"How 'bout if you come out and ask proper-like instead of yelling for the whole place to hear?" Geema was scrubbing a skillet. "It's ten o'clock in the morning. Goo-morning to you too!"

"Sorry, Geema." With one swoop, he kissed her saggy cheek and whisked away two strips of bacon and a cold piece of toast. He stuffed his face as he ran off.

"Just where in tarnation do you think you are going?" she yelled.

"Shishing. Botta bo."

"Stop right there, young man. Now, come back here and give your ole' Grandma the time of day. Try again."

He swallowed. "I'm goin' fishing, but I'm late so I gotta go." He punctuated the sentence with a pleading look. Geema shook her head up-and-down indicating permission, then side-to-side indicating exasperation. Dolby started to run away again.

"Oh, Dolby?"

"What?" He turned impatiently.

"Don't you need some fishing gear?" He had forgotten because fishing was the last thing he was about to do that morning.

Adele and Steele and their bikes had been waiting at the shower house. Dolby labored to breathe after his short ride. "Sorry." He didn't wait for a response but pedaled past them toward the lake. "Did you guys hear if they ever found Dee?"

"My mom said they found him last night after the parade. He had gotten lost on his bike and ended up at Gomer Ranch." Gomer's Hideaway Campground and Gomer Ranch, both owned by Veep, were located right next to each other on the outskirts of town, so Dee's getting lost was an easy mistake. Steele and Adele followed behind, content to let him lead, until they began to question his sense of direction.

"Dough-boy—this is not the way to the lake."

"Yes, it is. It's the back way—around the other side." They didn't see him pull out a small, metal whistle from under his shirt. They also didn't hear it because it was a special whistle that could only be heard by animals able to detect high-pitched noises. It was supposed to only be used in emergencies, but the line between real emergencies and perceived ones had blurred for the Half-tail lately. They arrived at a clearing that was hidden by thick woods on all sides and was covered with weeds except for a circle of bare ground in the middle.

"What are you doing, now?" Adele asked as they dismounted the two-wheelers. He didn't have to answer. Once a black-tailed buck, a red deer, a Rocky Mountain Elk, and two does arrived, she knew enough to answer her own question. "Is this like the Circle of Nod?" Dolby smiled. "Ugh. This has gone too far. You are paranoid, Dolby. There *is* no threat. It's as if you are making up dangers so you can be Half-tail again. I give up. You talk to him." Adele was looking for support from Steele.

"If you need us, we're goin' fishing," sighed Steele.

"Nice talk, Steele," said Adele sarcastically.

Red Velvet, the red deer, Shadow Muzzle the Elk, and Snowflake all sat down around the perimeter of the circle. Speckles, a friend of Snowflake's and about the same age, ran around the animals as if about to play an intense game of *Duck, Duck, Goose*. "This is Circle of Nod, isn't it? My first one! Circleofnod! Circleofnod! Circleofnod!" He stopped when Monster Horn snorted a massive, mean-sounding wheeze.

"More like Semi-circle of Nod, ay Dolby?" Monster didn't seem happy. Speckles took his place in the ring. Shadow Muzzle stomped his front hoof.

"What's a'matter with you guys?" asked Dolby, sensing the tension.

Shadow Muzzle, the usually dutiful bodyguard, spoke first. "This be fourth time Half-tail call council in last thirty moons . . ."

Red finished the thought. " . . . and each time it has been a false alarm of some imagined danger that you've made up in your mind."

"This time is different, though."

Snowflake piped up. "Is it? Because if I could be honest, bud, there is no danger in the winds. Nothing at all in the air."

Dolby wasn't used to Snowflake telling him things he didn't want to hear. "Just like last time."

"Except that last time our water supply was drugged and we lost our sense of smell."

"What about foreign visitors? Any deer from faraway lands showing up in Gomer?"

"Not even one."

Dolby was missing all of his old friends like the elk—Canuck from Canada and Wapiti from California—Mortimer the Moose, Zayan and Saluja, Sambar Deer from far-away exotic lands, and of course, Fantasma, his mysterious albino mentor. As he thought about his deer friends who traveled to Gomer for the great battle, he knew he was forgetting someone. Was it Princess? Raindrop? No, they were still around. Who was he forgetting?

"HOW DO! Well, butter my butt and call me a biscuit! Dolby Hart! Ain't my face grinnin' like a possum eating fire ants."

"GUS!" Dolby hugged the Mule Deer. "You came back!" He jumped into the middle of the circle and began to pace around with nervous energy. "See, I told you something is happening. Gus is the first one blown back by the winds of the Windmaster. It's the beginning of something big. I just know it!"

"What in thee Sam Hill?" came the reply. "I don't know 'bout all that mess. I just been roamin' the countryside—been busier than a one-legged man in a butt kickin' contest—and thought I'd come back to say howdy. That's all. Reckon I wasn't sent here like before."

"Well, you'll see. Something's up, and I intend to find out what, before the what finds us." Dolby continued. "But there is something I can't seem to figure out."

"What's that?" asked Red. They were already there so they might as well hear what he had to say.

"I talked with a guy, um, a no-tail yesterday who acted like maybe he knew I could communicate with deer. At least I thought that's what he was saying. It wasn't clear. But, I'm not sure because how could he possibly know? There's only a handful of people who know my half-tail abilities, and they promised never to tell anybody."

"Who all knows? Tell us! Tell us!" Speckles couldn't contain his excitement at being included.

"Ok, let's see. Mom, Geema, Adele, Steele, and the deer of Gomer. That's it."

The Semi-circle of Nod was as quiet as if they had actually nodded off to sleep. Shadow Muzzle finally broke the silence.

"Shadow have idea. You forget one who is important."

"Who's that Shadow?"

"Somebody we put in cage!"

All at once, everybody shouted, "Mrs. Krantz!"

Dolby thought for a second. "True, but she is safely behind bars with her husband. They can't tell anyone."

"But they can," chimed in Red Velvet. "Aren't no-tails allowed to visit others who are caged?"

Dolby replied, "You're right. You are right! You're on to something. Maybe she is plotting something from prison to destroy all of us once and for all. If she spent forty long years plotting her revenge against the white-tail, she's not going to give up now, even when locked up. She could be meeting with visitors to carry out some plan. Looks like I'm going to have to pass go and go directly to jail." The animals all shifted their heads in confusion. "Oh, sorry. It's a no-tail thing."

8

PIZZA

"Alone—it is wonderful how little a man can do alone."

—H.G. WELLS IN *INVISIBLE MAN* (1897)

"So, my plan is to pretend like I'm doing a report for school, get an interview with a guard or officer, and then come up with some excuse for them to leave me alone. When they are gone, I'll grab the visitor's log and take pictures with my phone to find out if anyone has been visiting Mrs. Krantz. I'm pretty sure they have visiting hours on Saturday mornings, so let's go!" No part of the Semi-circle of Nod budged.

"Not this time, Dolby." Red spoke for the whole group. "There is no good reason to go chasing down something that isn't there."

"Are you kidding me?" cried Dolby. "Fine. Snowflake, you coming?" Snowflake looked away.

"Great. I didn't need any of you in this plan anyway. You'll thank me later." For a moment, Dolby thought about heading to the lake to see if Adele and Steele wanted to watch him work, but all he could picture in his mind was a *Gone Fishin'* sign. "Go fish, then. Some supportive friends you turned out to be."

Dolby parked the Huffy against the outside brick of Gomer County Jail. It felt good to allow the door to slam behind him. He really wasn't very prepared for the plan because he was too busy fuming about how everybody was treating him. He was the great Half-tail after all. After introducing himself to a female officer behind a desk, he quickly located the visitor's log front and center on the counter. He then casually mentioned that he had a school project and needed to interview someone about the jail.

"I'm happy to answer questions," replied the middle-aged woman looking down at Dolby over bifocals that had slipped down her nose. "But isn't school out already?"

Dolby froze but gathered himself to reply, "Um . . . yes . . . but this is for an extra credit summer project."

The officer squinted. He felt like she was peering into his soul.

"So, where is the pad and paper, then?" She had spent her entire career dealing with convicts, scam artists, con-men, and liars. Even though a boy of twelve-years old was in front of her, natural instincts kicked in.

Dolby's eyes shifted around quickly and he began to sweat. It felt like a minute, but he was able to finally hold up his phone. "I'm just going to take notes on my phone." He suddenly wanted to interview somebody else—anybody else. Besides, he wasn't going to get at the log if she was standing here talking down to him. "I'm sorry to bother you. You seem busy. Could you go and get somebody else that I could interview?"

She smiled. "Young man, I am not allowed to leave this office without someone manning the phones and the door. You've got all summer to write your paper, why don't you just go home and come back when you've got your story straight?" The alarm of the door on his way out sounded an awful lot like a game show buzzer that sounded when someone answered incorrectly.

At the campsite, Geema laid out items for lunch on a covered picnic table—pepperoni, mozzarella cheese, onions, green peppers, bacon, pizza sauce, and bread. When he saw the long-handled cast-iron pie cookers, he knew they were having mini-pizzas over the fire. "Hello honey! We are almost ready. I've got plenty for your friends. Weren't they coming for lunch?"

"They were, but I think maybe they got a better offer." Dolby had been humiliated just enough to send him spiraling into self-pity.

Geema opened up a pie iron, inserted two buttered pieces of bread, and handed it to Dolby. As he filled the pouch with pepperoni, bacon, sauce, and cheese, he began to also fill his grandmother in on what had happened. Twenty minutes later, when the coals were nice and ready, Geema felt ready for an analysis. She grabbed a stick and separated one lone piece of glowing coal from the rest of the burning pile. She plopped her own sandwich maker right on top of the mound of glowing embers but grabbed his and set it on top of the single coal. "Now take a load off." He obeyed. "Sounds to me like somebody has gotten too big for his britches. I believe your friends are tired of being treated like inferiors who are not needed. You started out like a military private—a nobody— and became a captain among other captains to achieve victory together. Somewhere along the way, you turned into an ornery, old general who just barks orders and expects everybody's blind obedience. Don't be surprised when your friends don't want no part'a that." She flipped her pie cooker over and motioned to Dolby to do the same. "Look, there's a reason the good Lord took one look at poor ole' Adam and said, 'it is not good that man should be alone.' We are designed to be with each other; we are designed to work together; we are made to use our abilities and gifts together for him and his purposes. You can't do this alone, Dolby. You need me, you need your mother, you need your friends, and most importantly . . . you need God." With that, Geema removed her pizza iron from the glowing coals, and unfastened the clip. Her cooker creaked open to unveil a perfectly browned, pizza sandwich. She motioned to Dolby to do the same. When he unhinged his iron and opened it, the bread was still as white as when it went in. He lifted one piece of that bread to reveal cheese that was not yet melted. The boy looked down at his one piece of coal. Not only did it look lonely apart from the other lumps of coal, but it was no longer red with heat. It was as black as if it had never been lighted. "See . . . our lives are like the campfire coal. As long as we stick together, we will burn hot for Jesus and we will be useful to him and his kingdom. But the second we remove ourselves from our brothers and sisters, our fire dies out and we quickly become of no use to anybody. Sonny, you may have unique abilities that others don't, but if you consider yourself better than them because of it, then you're not gonna be worth a hill-a-beans. Your fire's gonna die out lickety-cut."

"Thanks, Geema. You're right as always."

9

JAIL

"It is my duty, said he, to distrust mine own ability,
that I may have reliance on him that is stronger than all."

—JOHN BUNYAN IN *THE PILGRIM'S PROGRESS* (1678)

After clean-up, Dolby decided to go for a bike ride alone to think more about what Geema had said. He headed in the direction of the lake in the outside chance that Adele and Steele were still there. He had some apologizing to do. They were nowhere to be found so he skipped rocks instead. Each time the flat rock skimmed the surface of the lake, a ripple effect occurred—a ring appeared on the water that got bigger and bigger and spread out to the rest of the lake. The ripple effect. Dolby thought about that and asked for God's forgiveness for his selfishness and the ripple effect on others that it produced. He still really thought that there might be a clue at the jail but was now understandably more cautious. He knew he could not do it alone. He needed at least one other person's help. At that moment, Speckles came bouncing toward him as if on a trampoline. "Hi Dolby! Just came to say hi!"

"Hi Speckles!" It was hard not to be happy around the young buck—his enthusiasm was contagious. "I have a question I've wondered ever since you loST YOUR SPOTTTTTTSSSS." The deer sprinted away mid-sentence and was now racing through the tall weeds. Dolby waited for him to return. "Ihaveaquestion," he said as quickly as possible before he leaped away.

34

"Yes, Dolby?" Speckles finally stopped.

"You were named Speckles when you were a newborn because of your many white spots. But now that you are older and your spots are gone, don't you feel like Speckles is kind of a baby name?"

"Never thought about it before. I guess names don't matter if you are content with who you are on the inside. And I love the name Speckles!" His moment of maturity was immediately followed with an immature demand. "Time me!" he yelled as he sprinted away. It was while spending time with Speckles that the idea came to Dolby. This time he couldn't do it without his new friend.

It was late afternoon which Dolby knew was probably toward the end of visiting hours at the prison. Of course, Speckles was a willing participant—it was becoming clear that he would do anything for Dolby, the mighty Half-tail. Actually, it was becoming clear to Dolby that Speckles would probably do anything for anybody. Speckles was running circles non-stop around the moving black Huffy bicycle. He also talked non-stop. "'Member when you fought those monster wolves from the treehouse? That was awesome! 'Member when Monster Horn pulled you up out of danger behind the mill? That was awesome! 'Member when you sent the wolf half-tail and her no-tail husband to jail? So awesome! 'Member when . . .'"

Dolby interrupted. "Ssshhhh. We're almost there. You stay hidden in the woods until I give you the cue." He strolled up to the side of the building and motioned for Speckles to go. The one-year-old deer hopped quietly around the other side of the jail building where a dozen or so employees sat outside enjoying a break in a fenced-in area. Some were smoking; some were eating; but all were enjoying the nicest day of the year so far. Wapiti, the Tule Elk from California, used to joke with Dolby that Michigan had two seasons—winter and July 4th. It was a funny joke, but wrong about this particular May day. After a running start, Speckles jumped over the chain-link fence and into the courtyard with all the unsuspecting no-tails. Once in the enclosure, he began to run around as if confused and trying to figure out how to get out. Men and women alike screamed while scattering toward the building to watch through the windows. One female officer opened the fence gate while a couple of larger guards tried to corner the deer in order to force him toward the way out. During all of the chaos, Dolby snuck into the front entrance and looked for the woman from earlier. She was nowhere to be found—no doubt watching the mayhem somewhere nearby. Dolby opened up the visitor log and began taking picture after picture of pages going back to February when Mr. and Mrs. Krantz were first given a couple of rooms at the Graybar Hotel. Returning the log back to its original place and page, the boy detective slipped out without being detected. Speckles was still running around, slamming into the fence, and masterfully eluding capture. Dolby hid behind a nearby tree and bellowed in deer language, "Now!" At that, the deer stopped in its tracks, skipped right through the opening of the gate, and bounded away into the woods leaving two large men scratching their heads at what had just happened. The two sneaks met up at a previously determined location in the wood. This time it was Dolby's turn to repeat, "That was awesome!" over and over. He stuffed the evidence safely into his pocket and exclaimed, "Couldn't have done it without ya!"

Dolby heard the fish frying on the griddle for dinner but didn't stop to say hi. He went straight to his tent and pulled the zipper down for privacy. Both the notebook and cell phone were in his lap the second he sat down. Dolby crouched over the cell phone, scrolled through the pictures, and made notes in his journal. He looked like a forensics detective hunched over a microscope adjusting the knobs and looking for microscopic clues. The first surprise was to discover that only last names were used in the log, both for the visitor and the prisoner. He pored through four months of pages. Dolby's second surprise actually got the attention of others, too, due to the noises being made from inside the nylon laboratory. "Huh . . . Whoa . . . No way . . . Look at that!"

10

REUNION

"'Come sit with me, both of you,' she said.
'We'll talk of strange ice creams and such things as we seem to have a bent for.'"

—RAY BRADBURY IN *DANDELION WINE* (1957)

"DOLE-BEE!" sang Geema, "DINNER-TIME!" The family paused to pray. The only creatures who kept their eyes open were Dolby and Kit the fox; both were eyeing the fried fish still sizzling in the pan. Dolby loaded his plate with a sample each of Rainbow Trout, Walleye, and Smallmouth Bass. He didn't bother sampling anything else.

"Most kids his age don't like fish," Geema boasted to her daughter.

Karen also loaded up her plate. "Most kids don't have grandmothers who make fish this good."

Dolby plopped down on the picnic table and shoveled flaky fish into his mouth before others had even made their plates. "Mmmmm. Soooo good. Tastes fresh. Where did you even get it?"

"Where do you think?" Adele and Steele said together, appearing from out of nowhere. Dolby had forgotten already what they had left him at the Circle of Nod to do.

The boy lowered his plate and didn't know what to say. "Can . . . can . . . they stay for dinner?"

"They better since they're the ones who caught dinner!" Geema had already invited them. She wasn't quite serving the role of Cupid, but she *was* trying to bring people together in a similar way. Dolby caught himself tapping his foot to *In the Good Old Summertime* that was being sung across the campground. Despite the awkwardness, he was happy his friends had returned. After dinner, the friends walked silently to the camp store for ice cream. Before they left, Dolby made a point to grab his phone and notebook.

The three friends ate ice cream under a covered pavilion. They still hadn't said much to each other. Dolby broke the ice by breaking the ice cream. His second scoop toppled over onto the dirty picnic table. After a good laugh, Steele threw down the gauntlet. "I dare you to eat that right now without your hands!"

"Challenge accepted! Five second rule anyway!" Dolby lowered his face toward the scoop of chocolate but stopped short. "Oh," he exclaimed.

"What is it, Dough-boy—chicken much?!"

"No, it just smells kinda funny, that's all."

"Lemme see," came the reply Dolby was hoping for. The former bully now lowered his head to smell the frozen treat, blind to the fact that he was about to be bullied himself. Waiting until his face was inches away, Dolby shoved his nose into the melting scoop! Steele screamed and rose up with brown dripping from his face. The scoop was still stuck to his nose and cheeks. He plucked the ice cream off of his face and took off after Dolby. The two ended up on the ground wrestling in the dirt. Steele shoved the scoop into Dolby's face. Once sufficiently exhausted, the boys stood up laughing; each a dusty, sticky mess. The sight of their chocolate faces caused Adele to erupt with laughter as well. After a satisfied sigh, Dolby was the first to speak up.

"I know I've been kind of . . ."

"A jerk?" finished Steele.

"Yeah. A jerk. I . . . I . . . guess I . . ." Dolby struggled to find the words.

"We know." Adele was always saving the day. "How about we just forget it and move on?"

"Okay by me. Look, I know I've been jumping to conclusions lately. But I do value your opinions. I'm not sure if it's anything, but I have to ask what you think. Am I being paranoid again, or is this something to be concerned about?" He pulled out the notebook. "So, it started with Veep. When he was driving around looking for Dee, he made a point to mention my friends."

"So, what's the problem with that?"

"I think he may have made a point to mention my *deer* friends. Then he winked. He wanted me to know that he knew my alter-ego."

"Are you sure?" Adele asked. "There's no way he could know. None of us has told anybody, and neither Geema nor your mom would have told anybody either."

"And we know the deer *couldn't* tell anybody." Steele stated the obvious.

"Right. But Shadow Muzzle wondered if Mrs. Krantz has been telling somebody from jail." Adele and Steele both thought that one over. "So, I snuck into the jail and took pictures of the visitor log to see if it's anything."

"The first time or the second?" Steele smiled. "Sorry, Geema told us about your first visit. So, you obviously found something, huh?"

"You're not going to believe it. There is no record of anybody visiting either Mr. or Mrs. Krantz for the entire time they've been in the slammer."

"What's surprising about that? They are both a million years old and never had any kids," said Adele. "I mean, well, except the one."

"You didn't let me finish, nobody visited *except for one person*. Starting in February, there has been one visitor on many Saturdays, with the frequency increasing to every Saturday for the last month and a half."

"You're killing us! Who is it?" The suspense was eating at Steele.

"Barney Vanderflunder!"

"Haha. Seriously, who is it?"

"Seriously . . . it's Mr. V!"

"No way. Can't be! Unless Gomer is the last stop for Old Fart felons," commented Steele.

"So much for being a part of the Greatest Generation." added Dolby.

"First Mrs. Krantz and now Mr. V? He's got to be seventy years old or more. There's gotta be another explanation," added Adele.

"Think about it—Mrs. Krantz worked for Principal Vanderflunder for probably forty years as the school secretary, and I think they even knew each other before that. So, as close friends for some fifty years, isn't it possible that he could be carrying out her plot since she cannot anymore?" Dolby clearly had benefitted from having more time to get used to the idea.

"That's so far-fetched," admitted Steele. "He's always been a good dude, despite all the trouble I got into. Besides, he's not capable of any master plan—you know he would just Vanderflunder it."

"Okay, just think about it. I'm not totally convinced either, but just look at the log."

Adele scrolled through the pages. "Yep. The official visitor's log doesn't lie. *Vanderflunder* is right there in blue and black ink." She would not have believed it if she hadn't seen it with her own two eyes.

That night, another name was added to the suspect list. This one, however, included the first plausible motive.

Suspects	Reasons for suspicions	Possible motive
1. Enid Schwartz—lunch lady	—always rude 2 me —serves food so bad could be poison	—???
2. Mildred Snodgrass—librarian	—rude 2 me	—???
3. Jed Calhoun—Turkey-town Owner	—big deer hunter	—suspects Steele involved in the killing of his turkeys
4. Chief Kowalski—police chief	—rude 2 me —reputation 4 being corrupt	—???
5. Percy V. (Peev)—campground manager	—rude 2 me —creepy, big hunter	—???
6. Bones—night watchman	—rude 2 me —creepy	—???
7. Miss Daken—6th grade teacher	—nobody is that nice	
8. Barney Vanderflunder—middle school principal	—multiple visits to Edith Krantz	—2 seek revenge 4 Edith while she's in jail?

11

SNAKE

"God's grace is like a caterpillar in a ring of fire.
The only deliverance is from above."

—MARTIN LUTHER (1525)

The three friends hadn't talked anymore about the newly discovered evidence for a couple of reasons. First, every gear in each of their brains was working overtime trying to make sense of another attack by another old fogey. The second reason was named Hope Mitchell. She was a classmate of Dolby and Adele, although was a year ahead and going into eighth grade in the fall. It was unusual to see Hope at anything like Hideaway Campground because she was a top-notch athlete who was constantly training for this sport or traveling for that one. In fact, she was running wind sprints under the lights of the baseball field to get ready for an AAU basketball tournament. They didn't normally run in the same circles, but the combination of the boredom of training and what the kids were carrying attracted her like a deer to a salt lick. Dolby had waited two days to finally get out the fireworks that were burning holes in his backpack.

"Can I watch?" panted the sweaty newcomer.

"Of sure," stammered Dolby. He wasn't used to talking to pretty, popular, older girls. "I mean, of course. Do you know Adele and Steele?"

"I've seen you both around. Hi!"

Dolby unzipped his bag and dumped all kinds of different shapes and sizes of pyrotechnics onto the ground. Steele began twisting a lead pipe into the dirt—his way of trying to get his favorite bottle rockets shot off first. Before Dolby could even grab his matches, Hope shrieked.

"Ah! A snake!" Hope may have been a courageous athlete on the court, but off the court it was a different story. "I don't know if I like this camping thing," she said while hiding behind Steele.

Adele smiled as she snapped up the harmless snake with finger and thumb behind its head. There were still some places where farm girls had the advantage, she thought to herself. "It's only a Milk snake. It won't hurt you unless you are a mouse or rat."

"Hold on . . . I have an idea." Steele began digging holes into the dirt to form a small circle. "Give me those mini-cone fountains, Dough-boy." He handed him eight of the cones that, when lit, shot flames up into the air. Steele shoved them deep into the holes so that just the tips of the cones were exposed to the air. "I wanna see what it'll do when it's surrounded by fire!" After Dolby lit each wick, Steele gestured to Adele to drop the snake in the middle of the ring of flames. The snake wriggled around in circles trying to locate an escape route. Finding none, it curled up in the middle and twitched. Hope didn't like the reptile but did feel a little sorry for it.

"Stop! Save it!" She wasn't as used to using critters as entertainment as they were. "Save it, Steele!"

Of course, Steele had a new target for his fun. "You save it!" He wanted to see what she would do.

Hope only mustered up enough courage when she saw that no one was moving. She used a stick to slide the snake toward one wall of fire. Realizing that pushing it through the flames wasn't going to work, she finally yelled, "How?"

"You have to save it from above," advised Dolby, pointing up and over the tiny blaze. A thought ran through his mind at that moment—salvation comes from above. Rescue comes from above. Sounds like something Geema would say in one of her lectures. With a flick of her stick, Hope launched the tiny serpent up and over the fire and watched it slither away into tall grass.

"I did it! I did it!" Hope celebrated as if she had just kicked a game-winning goal. This was all new to her. Dolby had the presence of mind to quickly light the wick of a few Roman Candles in order to punctuate her small victory with an explosion of color and sound. The celebration didn't last long, however, as a different explosion was heard from another direction. A weasel of a man rolled up quietly in a golf cart and yelled, "STOP! STOP THAT! Fireworks are not allowed in this campground."

With the discovery of Mr. V. as the leading suspect, Dolby was no longer scared of Peev. After an eye roll, the boy asked, "Since when?"

"Since when I said so," came the reply. "I told you I'd be watching you." The phrase that once caused fear was no longer threatening. Dolby now saw that it was just a sad little power trip for someone desperate to be respected. "No more fireworks, got it?" Peev pointed and glared as his funny, little vehicle spun out and away.

"Speaking of snakes . . ." grumbled Steele.

"At least he's as harmless as a Garter snake," answered Dolby.

The four loaded up the backpack and filled a trash bag with the few empty fireworks shells they were able to enjoy. On their way back to the campsite, Hope ran ahead with the bag of trash to throw into a dumpster. She opened the plastic lid, tossed in the grocery bag, and screeched once again. She slammed the dumpster cover back down with a bang and stomped away yelling, "I *know* I don't like this camping thing."

"What is it?"

"I don't know. It was too dark in there to tell, but I definitely heard a loud hissing. Is it another snake?"

Steele replied, "There's only one way to find out." Dolby handed Steele a flashlight from his bag and he approached the trash receptacle like a policeman about to barge into a criminal's house. He tossed open the dumpster lid, shined the light inside, and stepped back. "Yep. We've got a hisser," and handed the flashlight to Adele and Dolby, who confirmed what he saw.

"It's not a snake, Hope," said Adele. "Look for yourself." Hope cautiously peeked in and saw a fat, masked varmint cornered inside baring its teeth.

"See, it's only a raccoon." said Adele.

"Ugh. Ugly one, too. Are there more around here?" Hope suddenly fantasized about the safety of a gym.

Steele laughed. "Yeah, this place is covered with them—infested might be a better way to put it. I guess it's all the food laying around from campers because Gomer Ranch and other places aren't swarming with them like here. Stupid trash pandas."

"That's what I called one of them the other day," chuckled Dolby. "I guess you're rubbing off on me." Just then, another flashlight appeared, and another hiss was heard, but this time from Bones.

"Let's move along. Nothing to see here. It's almost curfew time," sneered the night watchman.

"It's not even ten o'clock," mumbled Steele under his breath. "Wait." Steele never heard of a curfew at the Hideaway before. "Mr. Bones, is there really a curfew?"

"Naw. That's just what Mista Peevs done told me to tell any lolligaggers. But I reckon I shouldn'a tole y'all that, huh?" Bones grunted and continued his night patrol with half a donut in hand.

Hope's heart was still racing faster than during a Track and Field event. "Man, this place is covered with snakes, raccoons, and who knows what else?'

"Also, frogs," Adele added as a punch landed on Steele's arm.

The barbershop singing grew louder as they got closer to their respective campsites. Hope felt awkard asking, but before parting, she wondered if they could hang out the next day. Dolby wanted to dig more into the whole Vanderflunder lead, so wasn't sure about spending time with her. "Maybe. I know Geema loves to go to outdoor church, but after that I might be free." They shuffled quietly in the dark. "Goodbye, My Coney Island Baby."

"Excuse me?" said Hope.

"Oh, sorry." Dolby blushed and pointed at a foursome singing away. "That's the song they're singing." After such an embarrassing confession, Dolby thought that it was entirely possible that Hope wouldn't want to hang out with them tomorrow after all.

12

S'MORES

"His habit is to move in mystery, yet sometimes He permits us
to think we see and understand Him."

—LEW WALLACE IN *BEN HUR: A TALE OF THE CHRIST* (1880)

Now safe together out of everyone's earshot, including Hope's, the three friends huddled in a two-man tent discussing Barney Vanderflunder. Dolby was ready with pen and paper to write down every scenario, every idea, and every theory that they could possibly think up. Unfortunately, the paper remained blank to match their brains. There truly was nothing to go on with regard to a deer attack at the hands of old Barney. Even Snowflake and Speckles joined the pow-wow, except they remained outside of the te-pee. Snowflake continued to insist that nothing out of the ordinary was in the winds. Could they be jumping to conclusions about what the elderly principal was capable of? Dolby had to finally admit that it was entirely possible.

"Who wants s'mores?" Geema's voice sounded like a dinner bell. Dolby marveled at how much of camping trips revolved around food. The kids tore out of the tent followed this time by two deer, who were careful to stay hidden in the shadows. They plunged their marshmallows into the heat and turned their faces away from the smoke at the same time. The kids took turns tossing marshmallows to the young deer lurking in the bushes. Dolby questioned himself every time he threw one to Speckles—he wondered what the effect of a bunch of sugar would have on one already so hyper. Of course, the traditional argument began about which level of cooked marshmallow was best. Geema and Dolby were on Team Brown, where the right answer was to roast the round sugar blob so that it was consistent all the way around with a golden, tan glow.

"When it's mushy all the way through it melts the chocolate the best—like so." Dolby chomped onto a s'more, which dissolved in his mouth, producing the inevitable *mmmmmm* sound.

Representing Team Black was Adele and Steele. "But only when it's burnt to a crisp do you get the real campfire taste," argued Adele with a crunch, her hands and mouth now sticky with sweetness.

"Besides, if you just burn the heck out of it, you also get to eat it faster," added Steele. The two deer were neutral in the debate. They just wanted more. Geema waited until the kids were silently occupied with chewing to do her own investigating.

"I think I'm gonna call it a night. Oh . . . and by the way, I happened to overhear you whispering about my friend Barney." Dolby continued to be surprised at how selective his grandmother's hearing always was. "Can I ask what all that yakking was about?" Dolby quickly sifted through his options. He decided in the end that it was better to come clean. Geema always had a way of knowing when he was lying. He told her everything he knew, which wasn't much. "Look, son. I think you are barking up the wrong tree here. I've known Barney for fifty years or so, and he simply doesn't have it in him to harm a flea. Besides, either something's wrong with your visitor log information, or somebody has doctored it up because . . . every Saturday you say?"

"Yep. Mrs. Krantz has been visited by him every Saturday for the last two months."

"Can't be. I know this for a fact. Barney and Sharon have a cottage on Lake Charlevoix and they spend every summer weekend there—have for years. Meets up with all their kids and grandkids. They got all kinds of toys up there—jet skis, paddle boards, paddle boats, pontoon boat. It's quite a spread . . ." Dolby rescued Geema from her rabbit trail.

"So, your point is?"

"He couldn't have been the one visiting Edith."

"Yeah, but do we have any proof that he's actually been there lately?"

"Well, Karen? Can you pull up the Facebook for a sec?" Dolby's mom was cleaning roasting forks.

"Sure . . . hold on."

"Show them Barney's page. He may be old, but he can still find his way around the internets."

Karen passed around her phone. Many posts and pictures from the lake house were time-stamped, often on weekends, which was proof enough to make for a legitimate alibi.

"But then I don't get it. Why is his name all over the log?" At this point, Dolby was thoroughly confused.

At that very moment, five reddish-brown Sitka deer were swimming across a river somewhere in Wisconsin. Fantasma often used Sitka as messengers due to their being smaller, more agile, and better swimmers than most deer. Sitka often live on islands, so they are accustomed to swimming across even the deepest channels of water. Because of their smaller stature, Fantasma would send them in groups for better protection. Traveling together for important missions also ensured that dispatches would get relayed even if one or two was unable to finish the trip. This particular group was known in deer circles as *The Albino Express* due to their being the communication team of choice for the wise Fantasma. Their assignment was simple. They were to carry an important message to the Half-tail himself.

Feeling defeated, Dolby reclined in his sleeping bag editing the notebook. He was no closer to discovering the truth than when he first started searching months ago. Maybe it was time to give up. Maybe he *was* just trying to relive his past former glory. Maybe he just needed to move on. Was it possible that his role as Half-tail to the whitetail was only to protect them from Mrs. Krantz the one time? Was his time in the spotlight over? He nodded off to a serenade of barbershop quartets, frogs, crickets, raccoons, and his own doubts. Little did he know that in less than ten hours, a squadron of Sitka would deliver a note that would change both his attitude, and everything else.

Suspects	Reasons for suspicions	Possible motive
1. Enid Schwartz—lunch lady	—always rude 2 me —serves food so bad could be poison	—???
2. Mildred Snodgrass—librarian	—rude 2 me	—???
3. Jed Calhoun—Turkey-town Owner	—big deer hunter	—suspects Steele involved in the killing of his turkeys
4. Chief Kowalski—police chief	—rude 2 me —reputation 4 being corrupt	—???
5. Percy V. (Peev)—campground manager	—rude 2 me —creepy, big hunter	—???
6. Bones—night watchman	—rude 2 me —creepy	—???
7. Miss Daken—6th grade teacher	—nobody is that nice	
8. ~~Barney Vanderflunder—middle school principal~~	~~—multiple visits to Edith Krantz~~	~~—2 seek revenge 4 Edith while she's in jail?~~

13

MESSAGE

"If I cease searching, then, woe is me, I am lost.
That is how I look at it—keep going, keep going come what may."
—VINCENT VAN GOGH
IN *THE LETTERS OF VINCENT VAN GOGH* (1914)

SUNDAY

Dolby's mother and grandmother took turns threatening Dolby to get up for church. His excuse was that he had stayed up too late reading. After bursting his bubble the night before about Mr. V., she suspected that the more accurate reason was good old-fashioned discouragement, and maybe even depression. But Geema was old-fashioned too and didn't put up with any of that nonsense. "Get up boy . . . I'm not going to tell you again. It's time for the preachin'. Come on—it'll be good for your soul."

At that moment, five swift deer leapt across state lines from Indiana into the great state of Michigan.

As they settled into their camp chairs under the covered pavilion for outdoor church, a Latvian girl from his school got up and sang a prelude solo which kept his interest for the moment. Her mom also kept his interest as she snapped picture after picture of the monumental event. After a prayer, four bald men who ironically no longer had any need for a barber, began a painful barbershop-style rendition of *It is Well with My Soul*. Dolby groaned as he sunk lower in his chair. The first thought to enter his head was that he couldn't escape it even in church. He sang quietly with the music— "It is NOT well . . . with my soul." Geema shot him a look. His next thought was that there was no way his elderly grandma just heard that. When it was actually time for the preachin', the guest pastor took the podium and read excerpts from 2 Chronicles 20 in his King James Version Bible.

> "O our God, wilt thou not judge them? For we have no might against this great company that cometh against us; neither know we what to do: but our eyes are upon thee . . . Thus saith the Lord unto you, Be not afraid nor dismayed by reason of this great multitude; for the battle is not yours, but God's."

Those words were the last ones that Dolby heard as his mind started racing elsewhere. He wondered if the message was directly for him. Was he going to face another great company coming against him and the deer? Was he to face another great multitude? Was another battle in his future? The only part that he could relate to was the statement that he didn't know what to do. The more he thought about it, the more afraid and dismayed he became. He didn't realize it, but he was completely missing the point of the passage. Not only was he getting more discouraged, he was also anticipating a personal battle, not one that was fought with reliance upon God. If the preacher was reading instead from the King Dolby Version Bible to reflect his current mindset, verse fifteen would have read, "for the battle is not God's, but yours."

Dolby's arms felt too tired to pick up the sandwich that Mom had made, so he didn't. He stared at his plate of food wondering why he had bothered at all over the past few weeks. It all led nowhere anyway. He was tired—tired of thinking; tired of looking for clues; tired of looking over his shoulder. He was also tired of his own need to do the next great thing. It was all exhausting and he was ready to give up no matter the cost.

Shadow Muzzle was only doing his job when he caught five Sitka deer watching Dolby under the cover of the pine trees. Monster Horn also came to Dolby's defense. The messengers weren't offended, just surprised. In all of their many campaigns, *The Albino Express* never encountered a security force, let alone one as secure as what the Black-tailed buck and Rocky Mountain Elk were currently providing.

The family decided to take a nice Sunday walk through the park and get some more wood for their campsite. They had a day and a half left at Gomer's Hideaway Campground before having to go back to reality again. Against their better judgment, they permitted Dolby to stay behind. They didn't know how to help him any more than he did. Fittingly, the acapella soundtrack to his blues happened to be a nearby group singing the spiritual, *Swing Low, Sweet Chariot.* The second they started, Dolby blurted out loud for nobody in particular, "perfect." Then, the second he felt random raindrops splatter on him, he exclaimed even louder, "just perfect!" Everyone around him darted for shelter, but Dolby remained slouching at the picnic table letting the rainstorm drown his sorrows. Dolby was in such a mental fog that he didn't notice Snowflake run right up behind him in the broad daylight. "What are you doing? Are you crazy?" squeaked the boy. He looked around. Thankfully, everyone was under shelter.

"Come on!"

"Where am I going?"

Snowflake didn't answer but led him on a beeline to the nearest woods. They were met by Speckles who was already jumping in place with excitement.

"There is somebody here to see you!" The two whitetail led Dolby to a tree-lined opening where they were met by Shadow, Monster, and five deer Dolby had never seen before. Each of the five newcomers bent their front, right knee at the sight of the Half-tail, making a synchronized bow of respect. They then formed a line and slowly approached Dolby. The leader lifted up his head and touched Dolby's nose with his nose. The rest did the same. It was then that Dolby realized they were of the Sitka species. Being greeted with Eskimo kisses reminded him that many Sitka come from cold climates like Alaska and British Columbia.

"I am Chinook," said the leader, "meaning warm wind." Chinook motioned to the rest of *The Albino Express* who introduced themselves. Chinook, though, translated the meaning of each name.

"They call me Panuk." ("Meaning *island*")

"I am named Qannik." ("In our language— *snowflake*"). The other Snowflake looked up with eyes sparkling.

"Suka." ("Which means *fast*.")

"Nanook." ("*Kind*.")

"We bring gentle greeting," continued Chinook, "from her wisdom Fantasma Bianca." A rush of joy flowed over Dolby just like a warm wind. "We swim rivers, climb hills, run plains. Many moons. Bring word from Fantasma, Wood Phantom." The five Sitka deer looked at one another as if enjoying the suspense and were pausing for effect. They seemed as excited to deliver the message as the Half-tail was to receive it. Chinook stepped forward. "Fantasma message to Half-tail. One word. *Nipisiuppuk*." The five deer each raised up their front legs as if doing a wheelie on a motorcycle and snorted and sneezed with approval. Dolby, though, didn't get it.

"I . . . uh . . . I don't know that word."

Chinook turned to his partners. Dolby heard more words that didn't mean anything to him. "Nipisiuppuk? Nipisiuppuk. Angunasuktuq? No. Kinik. Yes Kinik."

Chinook tried again. "Fantasma message—*Kinik*." Dolby still didn't understand. Now Chinook began talking to Shadow Muzzle. After a lengthy discussion, they all nodded in agreement. Shadow Muzzle finally turned to Dolby.

"Blacktail think message from Fantasma is closest to our word *hunt*."

"Angunasuktuq. Angunasuktuq," came the sounds from the Sitka.

"Blacktail think word like maybe *seek* or *search*."

"Nipisiuppuk! Kinik!" said the visitors.

"Wait. So, Fantasma bothered to send a troop of messengers over hundreds of miles and across many states to deliver to me a one-word message? And the message is *search*? Huh." Dolby didn't understand and knew to do only one thing. He inhaled a deep breath into his lungs and blew hard into his trusty whistle.

14

DISHARMONY

"This is a story about how a Baggins had an adventure, and found himself doing and saying things altogether unexpected. He may have lost the neighbor's respect, but he gained—well, you will see whether he gained anything in the end."

—J.R.R. TOLKIEN IN *THE HOBBIT* (1937)

Dolby was surprised to find the makeshift Circle of Nod still empty when he arrived. Normally when he blew his emergency whistle, they would be there waiting for him. After a few minutes, Shadow, Monster, Red, Snowflake, Speckles, and Gus all strolled in from different directions and leisurely took their places in the semi-circle. The deer had never heard the story of *The Boy Who Cried Wolf*, but were beginning to act it out in real life without even knowing it.

"This better be good," grumbled Red Velvet, "or else the next time you really need us and blow that thing, we may not come at all thinking it's nothing again."

"Oh, it's something all right!"

"Yes, but is it *emergency*?" growled Monster Horn.

"Well, I'm not sure if it's exactly an emergency, but I know you all will wanna hear this." Skeptical snorts filled the opening in the woods. "After four months, Fantasma has spoken!" All the deer sat up a little straighter and made eye contact with each other. "A delegation was sent from who knows where to deliver a message to me. But, it's awfully curious."

"What did they say?" asked Red.

"I mean, I didn't understand it at first, but Shadow was there—Shadow had to translate for me and . . ."

Gus interrupted. "So, get on wit' it—spill 'dem beans."

"What's weird is that she sent a one-word message."

"And?" Monster spoke for the rest of the impatient group.

"The one word is . . . *search*, or *seek*, or *hunt*. Something like that. What do you think it means?"

"We usually rely on Fantasma to decode puzzles and clues. Can't do that when she's the one sending the riddle," Snowflake correctly observed. "That is one weird message though."

"Yeah—nuttier than a squirrel turd." Gus always did have a way with words. Many animals took turns walking the circle, but in the end, nothing was really decided or discovered. Dolby's next move was to bring in Adele and Steele and maybe Geema and Mom. That familiar adrenaline was kicking in to be leader and hero again.

Dolby finally found them at the old campground putt-putt golf course. It was run-down and overgrown with weeds. But it was something to do on a lazy Sunday afternoon. Adele and Steele were one of the very few people on the course, unless you count the two little clueless boys on the 18th hole hitting the ball extra hard like they were teeing off at the Masters. The college kid working the desk saw them but couldn't be bothered while simultaneously watching golf on TV, listening to a podcast, and singing. Adele and Steele listened intently knowing that Dolby was trying very hard to be level-headed about all this business. "The only thing I can figure is that Fantasma knows something that I don't and doesn't want me to give up looking for clues, or villains, or possible attacks, or whatever. I say that because on Saturday night and Sunday morning I was ready to throw in the towel. But apparently I am not supposed to give up?"

"I guess," said Adele. "But one thing's for sure—if Fantasma is involved, there must be something to what you've been suspecting. I'm sorry I didn't take you more seriously. I will help more now."

"Me too," added Steele. "And even though she sent a message of just one word, it must mean something."

On their way back to ask Geema and Mrs. Hart for their opinions, Dolby first heard, and then saw, Hope practicing on the basketball court. She looked either dedicated or bored—he couldn't decide which. She was working on her Euro step layups. Because the three kids didn't understand much about basketball, her funny, two-step hop and shot looked ridiculous to them. Dolby felt bad, but he couldn't include her like she probably wanted. So, the three ducked behind the bathroom building and went the long way back to camp to avoid her. Unfortunately, Hope had seen them and was about to shout their names when they scampered off in the other direction.

Back at the campsite, the three kids were expecting some great nuggets of wisdom about the message; some new insights that they hadn't considered. But all they got were crickets. Not just silence from Karen and Geema, (they got that too) but *actual* crickets. The crickets that Dolby's mom had gathered for snacks for her pet fox had escaped after the jar tumbled. The scrambling of the kids to catch them made conversation impossible. Once enough of the insects were recovered to satisfy Mrs. Hart, she was off to treat Kit without even a thank-you. "What about the *search* message Geema?" Geema waited so long to answer, Dolby wondered if she was using her selective hearing again.

"Hear that?"

"Of course," came the exasperated reply. A singing group had just started bellowing *Sweet Georgia Brown*, a song made famous by the traveling basketball team, The Harlem Globetrotters. It made Dolby think about Hope and how they had ditched her.

"Sorry, Geema—still not a fan."

"I know, dear. Remember when I said that there were things to be learned from this style of music?"

"I know what you're gonna say." Dolby was still not terribly teachable.

"Do you, now? Then enlighten me, young man," she said with a condescending twinkle.

"You're gonna say that the four people in the group have to work to-gether in order to stay in harmony with each other. You're gonna say that there is not a lead singer in a barbershop quartet and that they all have to contribute their unique part to make it sound good. You're gonna say that like a quartet, I need to rely on others and God to help me in my life; that I can't do it alone. Stuff like that. Was I close?" Dolby had heard enough of her lectures that he was confident that he was.

"All good points. All worth considering. But I was taking it in an-other direction. I know nothin' about bein' a Half-tail, or messages, or oncoming danger—I just don't. I can't help you there. But what I do know is that when we come to The International Barbershop Competition, from Friday to Monday, from morning 'til night, we are surrounded by music. It is constant. I want you to think about that in your current dilemma, and in all future dilemmas. Because there is something that is always going on that you need to listen for—and that is God's voice and God's work. I believe it's in John where Jesus says, 'My Father is always working, and so am I.' Just like the music, wake up listening for it and go to bed letting it tuck you in. His guidance and direction are everywhere—in his beautiful world, through others, through daily circumstances, and especially in his Word. Spend your time seeking him and he will show you the way. I can say that because I have experienced it for most of my seventy or so years. When you are as old as I am, you can look back and see God's fingerprints all over your life." Dolby listened. He truly did. But he couldn't help to think that he and his Geema were simply in two different places in life. She was cramming for final exams, while he was just starting recess. Be-sides, he hadn't cracked open a Bible voluntarily outside of church in, well . . . ever. And if he was being honest, he wasn't about to. He had someone or something to search after.

15

PHONEBOOK

"A letter may be coded, and a word may be coded. A theatrical performance may be coded, and a sonnet may be coded, and there are times when it seems the entire world is in code."

—LEMONY SNICKET IN *A SERIES OF UNFORTUNATE EVENTS: THE BEATRICE LETTERS* (2006)

MONDAY

Since Monday was dedicated to family, fun, and fireworks, Dolby hadn't seen Adele, Steele, or even Hope. They, too, were all spending the day with their families. Also, since Monday evenings were dedicated to packing up and heading home, Veep and Peev traditionally made the rounds throughout the campground for very different reasons. Veep enjoyed seeing where he could be of use—helping elderly load their vehicles, showing new campers how to empty their RV bathroom's holding tank, or using his ample muscles to collapse a pop-up camper. Peev, on the other hand, barked orders and last-minute rules from his golf cart through a megaphone to make his life easier. He could be heard yelling things through his bull-horn like, "Move your picnic table back where you found it," or, "Clean your site. Don't leave it dirty for the next campers. Take out what you brought in!" Uncle Veep was the first to arrive to help Geema and her family. Of course, he carried himself in typical fashion—like a loveable mayor enjoying his constituents, or a doctor with an impressive bedside manner caring for his patients.

After Peev's drive-by verbal beating, Dolby commented, "It's hard to believe those guys are twins."

"Or came from the same parents," added his Mom. That's all Dolby needed to hear. All of a sudden, a thought occurred to him that he couldn't believe hadn't crossed his mind before.

"Um . . . Geema?" She answered with an exaggerated rising of both eyebrows. Dolby remembered that the names of the twins were Percy V. and Perry V. "What are Peev and Veep's last name?"

"Why, Vanderflunder, of course."

"They are Mr. V's *sons*?"

Geema chuckled. "Of course, dearie."

"Are you kidding me?" Dolby was saying this more to himself than to anyone else. He should've figured this out long ago. "So, the person visiting Edith Krantz in jail was a Vanderflunder after all? The last name in the log belonged not to Barney, but to one of his sons?"

Geema responded in a matter-of-fact way. "Certainly, dear. It's possible."

"Why didn't you tell me this before?"

"Well, I guess because you never asked." This changed everything. Peev could be the one Mrs. Krantz was pressuring to do her bidding against the deer of Gomer. His promise to always be watching him made him shudder once again.

"I can't believe I didn't think that the Vanderflunder of the visitor log could be anyone other than my principal. Wait until the gang hears about this!"

Hope was getting a quick jog in before leaving when she turned a corner and found herself face-to-face with Dolby who was himself running to tell any of his friends, tail or no-tail, of the recent development. It was an awkward confrontation. Dolby felt bad for avoiding her the day before. "Hey Hope."

"Oh, hi," came the reply. She had watched them run away from her yesterday and wasn't about to trust him again. Sensing this, Dolby invited her to join him in saying goodbye to Adele and Steele. He figured maybe he could speak in code in front of Hope. Surprised, Hope replied, "Are you sure you want me there? You obviously didn't want me hanging out with you yesterday." Dolby was surprised somebody so popular and pretty and athletic could also be so insecure just like him.

"About yesterday . . . um, it . . . uh . . ." Dolby froze like a deer in headlights. It wasn't unusual for him to freeze in the presence of an attractive girl. This time, however, it was because he was busted. "It just was not a good time. It doesn't mean we don't like you. Come with me, seriously. I could wait until you are done running?"

"No, I'm pretty much done. I guess I'll tag along." She was relieved. She was not used to being rejected and had the same fear of rejection that everyone has. Being a star athlete didn't change that.

Adele and Steele's tents were both on the other side of the park, so the new friends had to walk past many thickly wooded campsites. Hope began to notice more movement in the woods than was typical and mentioned it to Dolby. "Am I crazy, or are there more deer around right now?"

"Not sure. I haven't noticed."

Adele was waving goodbye to Uncle Veep, who had stopped by to help her and her dad put away their tent. As they passed by, he gave both Dolby and Hope an enthusiastic high-five. From two sites over, Steele joined the party. "Everybody headed home?" he asked. "Oh, hi Hope."

"Pretty soon," stated Dolby. "But I wanted to make sure I told you something before you left." He said it with eyes bugged out as if to indicate that he was about to speak in code. Adele nodded with understanding. "So, you know that old phone book I found? The one with only last names in it?" Adele nodded but Steele couldn't hide his confusion. "Well, turns out it is quite valuable."

"How so?" asked Adele, who was tracking his thoughts perfectly.

"Phone book?" asked Steele, who was clearly not. "What phone book?"

"So, it contains some surprising information." Dolby quickly felt ashamed that he had stooped to this level when he could've just waited to inform them back at home when Hope was not around. But he was in too deep to turn back now. "There's an error in the last names that start with *V*. There should have also been two sons listed under a man whose last name starts with *V*."

It was now Adele's turn for her eyes to bug out. "Oh, you mean . . . twin sons who share the same last name starting with the letter *V*?"

"Yes!" smiled Dolby. "And one of the sons is actually the one in the phone book. The father was included by accident." Both Steele and Hope looked at each other with the same puzzled look. Hope concluded that this was how all nerds spoke to each other.

"Wait!" cried Steele. "What phone book are you talkin' about?"

"I'll explain later," winked Adele. Hope didn't care that she didn't understand. She was just glad that she was being included.

16

RAID

"No one ever told me that grief felt so like fear."

—C.S. Lewis in *A Grief Observed* (1961)

The first free day after airing out the tents, unpacking, and mowing the lawn was spent down in the old, cold, abandoned coal cellar underneath what used to be the Dew Drop Inn. Their battle headquarters had gone basically untouched since Half-Tail Triumph. The only things different were more cobwebs, and more visitors to the mouse and rat traps. Steele tossed a stale Cool Ranch Dorito into his mouth to the horror of Adele. "You know that's probably been here since February." Steele ignored her as he copied Dolby's suspect chart onto the white board that was still leaning against the rock wall and resting on the hard, dirt floor.

Steele didn't waste any time. "So, we know a Vanderflunder spent a LOT of time with old Edith at Con College, and we know it wasn't Barney."

"That leaves Perry Vanderflunder and Percy Vanderflunder," offered Adele. Steele and Dolby both laughed. "What's so funny?"

"Did you just hear yourself?" scoffed Steele. "You made it seem like we have narrowed it down to two equally possible suspects. Think about it. Between the two brothers, which one is the more obvious choice to be involved in something dark and criminal?"

Dolby piped in. "Besides, how long have we known those two? One has a lifelong record of doing good in the community, and the other has a deserved reputation for being a snake. There's no question that if one of them is involved, it's creepy Peev for sure."

"I guess," replied Adele, "but what about Veep knowing that you are a Half-tail?"

"Well, I'm not even sure that's what he was implying. But I guess he could know without being involved with Mrs. Krantz. He could have learned it from his brother somehow, or from his Dad. Shoot, knowing Veep, he could have been visiting old Edith just to be a good guy and found out from her. There's a lot of possible explanations."

"I guess any of those things are possible," said Adele.

"So, is it safe to say we are all thinking the same thing? Peevy and Mrs. Krantz are the ones that are doing all the talking, and it's not been about the weather."

Adele nodded, "But what are they up to?"

Dolby answered, "I think that's the *search* that Fantasma wants me to continue."

"How are we gonna do that from this dungeon?" Steele asked with a loud crunch.

"We can't, which is why we have to convince someone in our family to take us camping over the fourth of July weekend." This time Dolby wanted to be near the action not for selfish reasons, but was thinking instead about the welfare of Snowflake, Gus, and the rest of the herd.

"You're going to be blown away!" exclaimed Steele, as the threesome turned four were marching toward the treehouse tucked away in the woods. Talking about Hart Castle, as Dolby liked to call it, distracted Hope from the questions she had for Adele. Did she notice all the deer escorts trying to stay hidden around them?

"So, you and Adele helped build it?"

"Well, we helped," said Adele. "But my Dad, Steele's Dad, and Jed Calhoun did most of the work. Took us almost three weeks to finish."

As they got closer, cries of "No way!" and "Whoa!" and "Are you kidding me?" and "What the?" echoed through the pines. Only they weren't exclamations from Hope's mouth. She was stunned silent with mouth open staring at the scene while the boys and farmgirl did the shouting.

Other phrases that filled the hollow were, "NOOOO!" and "Why?" and ones that can't be mentioned. The first thing they saw was garbage littered all over the 360-degree deck. Furniture was dragged outside with stuffing hanging out. Frito-Lay bags were opened with food everywhere. Clothes were strewn over the railings. But the inside was even worse—cabinets were torn from walls; the mini-refrigerator gaped open and empty; the bunk beds toppled over with sheets and pillows ripped to shreds. The kids shook their heads with shock as they dodged comic book pages that were blowing around the inside of the treehouse thanks to the broken windows. It seemed like an eternity before anyone came to grips with the destruction enough to say anything.

"Either some animals really wanted some chips, or someone has a sick sense of humor," offered Hope. "Teenagers can be stupid."

"Or someone is trying to send a message," speculated Dolby.

"I don't know. It looks to me like maybe they were tearing this place inside-out looking for something that they never found," theorized Steele.

"Which made them so mad they ransacked it completely?" Dolby felt sick for the second time over his beloved treehouse. He didn't feel much like revisiting in his mind the previous fire disaster. It was his fault the first time. But this time was worse. It felt like he had been violated; like he had been exposed. He couldn't shake the image of Peev's twisted face and stumpy finger pointing directly at him; and he couldn't get the sound of his unsettling voice maniacally repeating, "I will be watching you. I will be watching you!"

Dolby slipped away to ask if any of the whitetail had witnessed or detected anything. Most of them were at the campground with Shadow and Red and Gus. The rest were in other parts of Gomer's many woodlands. No animal provided any leads.

It was against his better judgment, but the last thing Dolby did before an attempt to sleep that night was to add critical information in columns next to Peev's name in the journal.

The only change he made was to move items from Mr. V's row to Peev's, who now replaced Barney as his primary suspect.

Suspects	Reasons for suspicions	Possible motive
1. Enid Schwartz—lunch lady	—always rude 2 me —serves food so bad could be poison	—???
2. Mildred Snodgrass—librarian	—rude 2 me	—???
3. Jed Calhoun—Turkey-town Owner	—big deer hunter	—suspects Steele involved in the killing of his turkeys
4. Chief Kowalski—police chief	—rude 2 me —reputation 4 being corrupt	—???
5. Percy V. (Peev)—campground manager	—rude 2 me —creepy, big hunter	—2 seek revenge 4 Edith while she's in jail?
6. Bones—night watchman	—rude 2 me —creepy	—???
7. Miss Daken—6th grade teacher	—nobody is that nice	
8. ~~Barney Vanderflunder—middle school principal~~	~~—multiple visits to Edith Krantz~~	~~—2 seek revenge 4 Edith while she's in jail?~~

17

DREAMFINDER

"The LORD your God is with you, he is mighty to save.
He will take great delight in you, he will quiet you with his love,
he will rejoice over you with singing."

—ZEPHANIAH 3:17

The last time Dolby entered information into his journal, he was kept up at all hours of the night from a nightmare. Like that night, he couldn't sleep. The only difference between that night and this one was the nightmare, because he was every bit as afraid. He couldn't shake the feeling that he was always being watched; always being stalked; always in danger. He had dismissed Peev to his face and possibly angered him even more. What was he and the evil old bat planning and how were they plotting to get him out of the way? He stared up at the ceiling trying to find some way to turn off his anxious brain. He roamed the house. He ate two of Geema's famous molasses cookies . . . then he ate a third. His digital alarm clock was blinking 2:17 a.m. when he settled back into his room. Still wide awake, and still hearing the words, "I will be watching," he felt like his secret hiding spot was calling. He pulled back the loose corner of carpet behind the door. He then pried up a plank of wood flooring with a screwdriver to reveal his personal, makeshift safety deposit box. A few ratty old journals were hidden under the floorboards along with trinkets and knickknacks that only an elementary kid would think valuable enough to keep hidden. One by one he removed and inspected each item. When he got toward the far end of the hiding place beyond where he could see, he grabbed for one remaining item but came out with two. A faded Chinese finger trap won at a county fair was his target, but a colorful feather came with it. He knew that even his eight-year-old version of himself would have never deemed a feather worthy of stashing, so he reached even further under the floor up to his elbow. As he suspected, after all these years of first visiting Geema, and now living with her in the crickety old farmhouse, another treasure had been buried right under his feet. An odd, oblong feathered item was discovered and brought to the surface. As he turned it over to investigate, it was also turning over in his mind why this weird thing was so familiar. It was a hollowed-out section of a thick tree branch. It was surrounded by netting with feathers attached. Strings of colorful beads wound around what looked like a primitive half of a pair of binoculars. He wondered if monoculars are a thing. In fact, it reminded him a lot of dreamcatchers that were made popular by Native American cultures. It wasn't until he looked through the opening that synapses began to connect in his brain. "This is my Dreamfinder!" he said out loud. His mother had made it for him when very young to help him fall asleep. He remembered sitting on her lap and looking through it for sleep like a sailor desperately searching for land. He had forgotten the nurture and care that she once gave him exclusively but was now divided between him and her other sons and daughters from the fox kingdom. He remembered that she would read to him also. What he didn't remember was etched in permanent marker on the Dreamfinder's side. Written in his mother's handwriting were three Bible passages. Was that what she would read to him to help him get to sleep? He tiptoed down creaky stairs to retrieve Geema's fat, family Bible from the kitchen table where she started each day. Dolby's voice whispered the words of God in a closed bedroom hoping to relive some good, old memories. He was about to discover that God's word is alive and active and relevant to his current life situation, and not just something sentimental and nostalgic from a happier time.

"I am with you and will watch over you wherever you go."
—Genesis 28:15

Dolby thought of Peev's haunting words "I will be watching you." He wouldn't be a good grandson of Geema's if he didn't know that God was watching over him. But it always seemed like his watching was from afar. He noted that God says his watching is while he is with him. If that's truly the case, then why does he fear Peev's watching so much? He smiled to himself. If the God of the universe was with him and watching him, then the watching from Peev stopped being so threatening.

> "Psalm 121:2–4 . . . My help comes from the Lord, the Maker of heaven and earth. He will not let your foot slip— he who watches over you will not slumber; indeed, he who watches over Israel will neither slumber nor sleep."

Dolby could feel a wave of comfort flood his body. "If God is watching and never sleeps, I can go to bed without fear. Huh. Maybe the Bible really is relevant after all. Last one."

> "Zephaniah 3:17—The Lord your God is with you, he is mighty to save. He will take great delight in you, he will quiet you with his love, he will rejoice over you with singing."

Dolby was left with an image of a loving father singing a lull-a-bye over his child to gently lead him to a peaceful sleep. Tension felt like it was physically leaving his body. He crawled back into bed after replacing the contents of his personal safe. His last thought before nodding off were the words "I will be watching." This time, though, they were words of blessing and favor and joy from a perfect heavenly father.

The month of June went by without incident. It was either life returning to normal or a long calm before an approaching storm. Most agreed it was the former. Steele was busy working for his dad rescuing and rehabilitating dogs from illegal fighting rings. The Rescue Dog Coalition was always extra busy in the summer as dog fighting and gambling ramped up. Adele's work on the farm never let up no matter the season. Dolby had cleaned up the treehouse enough to use again. But, before he moved even one item, he took detailed cell phone pictures of the crime scene. He remembered Officer Robinson doing the same thing during his investigation of the destroyed birds at Jed Calhoun's Turkeytown. There still was nothing to go on about how or why the treehouse got trashed, however. As time went on, it became easier to believe that maybe it *had* just been some bored teenagers or hungry animals after all. He decided to start early on his summer reading for school in case anything happened at the campground during the July 4th weekend. The four friends had convinced Adele's parents to take a couple of days off at the farm to go camping. Hope was busy with travel basketball, or was it soccer workouts? Dolby could never keep track. Speaking of track, it could've been Track and Field conditioning, too. The other thing that was keeping her busy was keeping an eye on Dolby. Even though they had just started hanging out, she had to admit that it hurt her to not be included sometimes. She knew something was going on—she heard their whispers—but couldn't quite put her finger on it yet. She was not your stereotypical dumb jock, so it was only a matter of time before she would figure it out. Besides being a good friend, she would also prove to be an essential part of their detective team.

Dolby's only excitement that month was a late-night trash can raid that woke up the whole house. Steele was spending the night when they came upon the bandit. After he scurried away, Dolby rubbed his eyes and announced how much he hated raccoons. "Yeah," replied Steele, "they always remind me of an old-timey masked burglar who's snoopin' around where he's not wanted."

18

RAINMAKER

"'Well, hello, Peter,' said Lupin pleasantly, as though rats frequently erupted into old school friends around him. 'Long time, no see.'"

—J.K. Rowling
in *Harry Potter and the Prisoner of Azkaban* (2004)

FRIDAY

With five sets of hands helping, the Brown's pop-up camper and Dolby's two-man tent sprouted from the ground in no time—like weeds in a wheat field, as Geema would say. Hope was the only pair of hands missing. She needed them for dribbling, passing, and shooting in nearby Spring Arbor. The campsite was set up just in time for a quick snack and the evening activities. With a pool party for the kids, Bingo for the elderly, and a Cornhole tournament for everyone else, Gomer's Hideaway Campground was left mostly vacant except around the events center. It was an unusually hot beginning to July, so water activities were definitely in the weekend plans for the teenagers.

Everyone walked back together after sunset; the kids wet and shivering under beach towels and Clayton and Carol Brown arguing over who played the worst cornhole. Both pointed fingers at themselves. Back at the site, Clayton began working on the fire pit while Adele, Steele, and Dolby changed out of their bathing suits. The boys unzipped the tent and stood dripping first in water, and then in bewilderment. The contents of two previously unpacked duffle bags were now strewn all over the floor of the Coleman Sundome. They quietly took inventory not wanting to involve the Brown's quite yet. Nothing was left in the bags, but nothing seemed to be missing either. "I think somebody is looking for something, Dough-boy," observed Steele. Dolby panicked for a moment before realizing that everything truly valuable—his wallet, cell phone, house key, and whistle had been with him at the pool in his backpack. He made a mental note to remain vigilant in keeping his backpack with him at all times. His next thought was that there was no way either teens or animals had raided his treehouse.

"I think they've been looking for something for a while."

The boys could only hint to Adele that something unusual had happened. The fire wouldn't roast the hot dogs fast enough for Dolby and Steele, who each gobbled up two along with some cold baked beans—they couldn't even wait for the beans to warm. The boys retreated to the twelve-foot by twelve-foot screen house erected in the case of rain. Adele took the hint and entered the shelter with more ketchup on her face than was in her stomach. "What is up with you guys?"

"Just this . . ." Dolby showed her his most recent pictures. "Happened while we were at the pool." Adele gasped. "Somebody is definitely after something."

"That's what we think," said Steele. "Whoever it is didn't go through this screen house, your camper, or even the car, all of which were unlocked."

"Do you think it's creepy Peev?" Adele continued scrolling through the iPhone. "Wait—you took pictures?"

"Of what?"

"The treehouse."

"Oh yeah—I have before and after pictures."

"Any clues in here?" She continued sliding her finger from right to left. This time she had an audience.

"Wait. Stop," came the first voice from over her shoulder. "Right there. Notice anything?"

"Yeah," came the other voice. "Lots of comic books and journals all over the deck."

"Look closer," encouraged Steele.

"Don't see it."

"Me neither," said Adele as she zoomed in with two fingers. For some reason she was always in charge of the media presentations.

"Zoom out a little. There. See it?" His question was met by silence. "Dolby, you cleaned up the treehouse, right?"

"Kind of. Mostly. Why?"

"Did you happen to notice a difference between the condition of your old journals and your comic books?"

He thought for a moment. "Now that you mention it, the comic books were mostly fully intact, and I was able to recover them. As for the journals, though, lots of pages were ripped out."

Steele grabbed the phone and faced it toward Adele and Dolby. "See?"

"Huh. So, somebody is either after certain journal pages or the notebooks themselves." Dolby quickly unzipped his backpack and located all three of the notepads that he brought camping. The one with his list of suspects was still there. After an exhale of relief and another quick zip, he pulled the bag tight to himself. "We are pretty sure Peevy is behind this somehow, but how do we know for sure?"

"Looks like we have to set him up. Some kind of trap to catch the rat."

"What's the bait?"

"This cheese," smirked Dolby, holding up the backpack. "I'll remove the two notebooks that I'm currently using. The other is blank. If he wants what he thinks is my journal, then he'll have to steal this backpack." The other used journal included inspirational quotes that he had collected through the years. He loved adding new ones whenever he stumbled across them. Once in a while he'd read back through the quotes to regain perspective.

"We've got the rat and the bait, but we're missing the rat trap," summarized Adele. At that moment, a wet, black nose and white mouth and chin nudged through the screen opening. Snowflake and her shadow bounded in excitedly. Speckles kept repeating, "Half-tail! Half-tail! Half-tail!"

"Guys . . . you shouldn't be here," Dolby scolded while looking around.

"We were careful, and the no-tails are on a walk," came the response. "Whatcha doin'?"

Dolby explained. He also explained their dilemma of how to know when and where Peev will be tomorrow.

"Oh, that's easy." It was Snowflake's turn to come to the rescue. "Tomorrow is Tornado Rainmaker day." Dolby translated, but it was something new to him. They had no idea what the doe was talking about. "You know, Tornado Rainmaker." With that, Snowflake popped a wheelie in order to demonstrate. With front hooves making a circular motion as if driving a vehicle, she made a wailing sound like a siren. "I just saw Tornado Rainmaker over by the Ranch."

"Ah," the light bulb went on in Dolby's mind. He turned to his human friends. "Tornado Rainmaker! Tomorrow must be the Saturday for fire truck rides!" It was tradition at least once a year to give fire truck rides to the campground children. When it was especially hot, like it was going to be tomorrow, there was the added treat of getting soaked by the water hose. "Deer must think that the siren sounds like a tornado."

Steele jumped in. "So, we know where he will be tomorrow. We can find out what time it starts. But what we don't have is a plan." Adele asked for the backpack and looked it over and over. She smiled.

"I think I've got the plan."

19

SPY

"A trap seizes him by the heel; a snare lays hold of him.
A rope is hidden for him in the ground, a trap for him in the path."

—JOB 18:9–10

SATURDAY

It was almost showtime. The long, straight stretch of gravel between Gomer Campground and Gomer Ranch was already lined with adults and kids alike in bathing suits and towels. If Fire Truck Ride day was like a high school playoff game, then *wet* Fire Truck Ride Day in Gomer was like the Super Bowl. Dolby checked his phone—12:30 p.m. He was getting nervous that all the pieces weren't going to fall into place in time. The fire truck shoved off at 1 p.m.

"Backpack?"

"Check," answered Adele, with a zip of the bag.

"Towel?"

"Check." Adele stuffed it inside. Much of the contents were just decoys.

"Sunglasses?"

"Check."

"Baseball hat?"

"Check."

"Blank notebook?"

"Check."

He looked around for the most important item. "Hope?"

"Check!"

The answer came from behind him, spoken by a girl in game shorts and a warm-up top. On a whim, the kids texted Hope to see if she could fit their plans into her schedule. Fortunately, all of her games that day were in the morning. She was promised to be let in on the purpose of the plan at a later time. Again, she was just giddy to be included and didn't care to know at that moment. The kids figured that if the plan went south, her being in the dark would help protect both her and the plot. Crowds of children were lined up waiting for their turn on the red truck with *Engine Company No. 17* written on the side. Dolby made it clear who Hope was to be watching.

"You have one job. All you have to do is keep your eyes on him. That's your only job." Dolby was convinced that Peev knew him, Steele, and Adele, but not Hope, which is why she was chosen to be the spy. They took their place in line. Peev was in position. His role on Wet Fire Truck Day was to play the bad cop to Veep's good cop. Veep was the adoration of all the kids for his annual job of driving them to the Ranch—around the cul-de-sac in front, and back to camp—all while leading in song, telling jokes, throwing candy, and stopping to spray onlookers. Meanwhile Peev had to stop children from getting on in order to keep the number of kids on the vehicle within regulation. He did this all while at the front of the line, so he was forced to watch Uncle Veep get even more wonderful in everybody's eyes. Peev thought to himself that at least it was his idea to start Fire Truck Rides in the first place many years ago. It was supposed to cheer him up a little. As a little boy hugged Uncle Veep on his way onto the truck, he decided that it did not, in fact, cheer him up at all. Peev argued in his head that he was the manager of the campground and therefore, he should be the one to drive the truck. Sixteen children at a time could make the trip, with fifteen occupying the jump seat area where firefighters normally sit, and one next to Veep where the captain would sit. One incident summed it up perfectly. The truck was at its limit when a skinny, naughty girl pushed past Peev on her way to get sweets from Uncle Veep. She just finished telling him that her name was Susie when Peev had to pull her off of the truck. Veep had gotten a hug for doing his job. Peev got a bunch of hard pokes in the belly for doing his.

As Dolby got closer to the front, he watched Peev closely to see if he reacted upon seeing them. He didn't. He just looked to be in pain. Dolby took one step onto the stairs of the vehicle and turned, again, watching very closely for any kind of reaction.

"Mr. Peev, sir?" The bald man merely grunted. "Can you watch my backpack for me? I've got some stuff in there I don't want to get wet." Another grunt. He grabbed the strap as if in further pain. Dolby watched from the window and whispered to Adele, "Well, he didn't look very excited to take the bait."

Adele agreed. "But he may just be a good actor, too." From a distance, the backpack disappeared out of Hope's sight. She got closer. As she did, she witnessed Peev making a phone call. Or was he taking a phone call? She hadn't seen. Hope's vision was obstructed by a tall, blonde girl dancing and laughing with her friends like a crazy person. Hope couldn't push through. Now they were filming themselves and taking selfies. Ugh! Finally, she got close again. Peev was not there! She jostled her way through the crowd and caught a glimpse of the back of his bald head enter the camp office. She followed him in because she was supposed to keep her eye on him. It was just the two of them now together in the office. She realized she had nothing to say. It was hard to tell what was moving faster, her eyes looking for the backpack or the gears in her brain trying to come up with something believable. She didn't have to because Peev wrote something down and clicked off the phone.

"The bathroom is closed during fire truck rides."

"Oh, um . . . I wasn't looking for the bathroom." No backpack yet.

"Well, he's not available either." Peev was used to people of all ages trying to get close to his brother. "And he's not hiring right now." He was also used to people using him to get to his brother for work opportunities. Hope looked older than an eighth grader, but she certainly didn't look old enough to be looking for a full-time job. Hope thought to herself that he wasn't very bright. Because of that, she also thought that maybe she could still pull this off.

"No, I was actually hoping to talk to you." For the first time in the conversation, the rat looked up. For the first time, he also seemed to have time for her.

"Me?"

"Yes. Aren't you the manager of the campground?"

"Have been for thirty-three years. I was about your age when I started." He thought she was in her early twenties. She wasn't about to correct him.

"I'm a student at Michigan State and I am changing my major. I think I want to be a Park Ranger now, which is kind of like what you do, isn't it?" She was enjoying the challenge of having to think on her feet, and he was enjoying the attention.

"Kind of, but I work circles around those guys."

"That's what I thought. I was hoping you could steer me in the right direction so I could become a Forest Ranger when I graduate."

"Sure. The first thing is to make sure your new major will get you a job. What major are you switching to?"

Hope scanned the room for help. A green magazine with pictures of a bison, bobcat, and a bird on the front caught her eye. The name of the publication was *National Wildlife*.

"I think . . . Wildlife . . ."

"Management?"

"Yep . . . Yes. Wildlife Management."

"Perfect. That works. Okay, what kind of questions do you have?" He tried to look important and professional but failed in true Vanderflunder fashion when the computer keyboard fell crashing to the floor.

Fifteen minutes later, Dolby, Adele, and Steele exited the Rainmaker. Dolby looked frantically for Peev and his backpack to the soundtrack of the Fire Truck siren. The piercing noise added to his stress. He finally found one, but not the other. A high school girl at the front of the line was keeping it safe on her back. "Excuse me. That's mine," said Dolby in a confused tone.

The girl responded defensively with her hands in the air. "Peev asked me to watch it for you. You're welcome—Sheesh."

"Thanks." The next thing he saw confused him even more. Exiting the camp office building was Hope and Peev laughing together.

20

OLYMPICS

"Do I not destroy my enemies when I make them my friends?"
—ABRAHAM LINCOLN

"You had one job!" repeated Dolby. "Do you remember when I said that? 'You have one job!' Yes, I'm sure I said it very clearly—one job. Are you crazy? You could have—no you still may have—blown this whole thing for us all."

"You're not listening to me." Hope couldn't stop him. Even though she didn't know the whole story, she thought that maybe some things came out of her conversation with Peev that would be of help.

"Okay, I'm listening." He wasn't listening.

"He left his post right after you gave him the backpack. I followed him into the office to see what he was planning to do with it. I was following your orders to keep my eye on him at all times. So, I had no choice. But he never brought the backpack with him. He never opened it—I'm sure of it."

"I was watching closely, too, Dolby. He never reacted when he saw us; he never reacted when he got his mitts on the journal; He wasn't interested," said Adele.

"So, my cover-up was that I was trying to get into Forestry—he thought I was college-aged—and needed to ask him some questions. Believe it or not, he was actually very helpful once he realized I wasn't interested in Uncle Veep. I don't pretend to know what this is all about, but maybe here's some stuff that you can use?" She pulled out a piece of paper with notes on it. "One of the questions I asked was, 'what are the hours like?' He replied, 'It mostly changes from day-to-day, but there's always something to do. Saturdays are the busiest because we usually have the most campers. Plus, there's non-stop activities on Saturday to make sure go smoothly. I don't have time for anything else on a typical Saturday.' Does that mean anything to you?" Dolby was listening now.

"What else did you ask?"

This time she watched for Dolby's reaction. "I saw that he had a couple of mounted deer heads and antlers in the office." Sure enough, Dolby's ears perked up as if he himself was a deer. "On a hunch, I asked him if he was a big hunter." His answer was 'not really'—he pointed to the stuffed deer mounts and said that his brother had gotten those. I took that answer and ran with it and asked him how his relationship was with Veep. That's when things got real. He slammed his hand on the counter as if to end the interview, but then he continued." Hope looked down and read from her tablet word-for-word. "My brother doesn't care about anybody but himself, and I mean everybody, including his family. He is my boss, and that's about the extent of the relationship. He appears to be such a great guy, but I'm telling you, if he does anything for anybody else, it's really for him somehow. If he searches for a lost kid, if he drives a fire truck, if he calls a couple who is divorcing, if he visits someone in jail, he's got some ulterior motive for it."

"Let me see that!" Steele grabbed the paper and read it over out loud just to make sure. ". . . if he visits someone in jail, he's got some ulterior motive for it." Steele shot a look at Dough-boy and Adele. "Did he say anything else?"

"The end was odd too. He said something like since I'm interested in wildlife management, that I might like to see something of Veep's. In fact, he mentioned that my friends might be interested in seeing this too, and then he winked. Is that supposed to mean something?" The eyes of the other three darted back and forth at each other.

Adele was the first to break the tension. "Dolby, I think we are going to be making a visit to good old Peevy. Before we do, though, I think you and Hope need to have a heart-to-heart." Dolby shook his head as if Adele was reading his mind.

"I agree, but let's make an appointment first. Hope, can you go find Peev and see if we can take him up on his offer? Maybe even later today if possible?"

"Sure. He gave me his number to set it up. Don't worry. I know what you're thinking. I don't think he is being creepy. It honestly seems like he's just happy to be talking to somebody." It was 3 p.m. and it worked for Peev to meet them at 7 p.m. Before he hung up, he emphasized to Hope that she bring all of her friends, with the emphasis on *all.*

Instead of telling Hope about his special ability, he thought maybe it would be best to show her first. But it made him nervous. The last time he tried to deliberately show someone his gift, he ended up humiliating himself in front of Adele at her farm. He pushed through knowing this was different. He was showing off before. This time he was including her for a bigger, more crucial, purpose.

Dolby led Hope past the basketball court, past the shower building, under the high ropes course, and to the open area reserved for deer meetings. After telling her not to be scared, he put his hands to his mouth and shouted in a deer grunt, "No-tail friend! No-tail friend here!" He sounded like the weirdest snack vender at the weirdest ball game. She heard the thundering from a distance. She heard it get closer. She heard the surrounding forest come alive with noise. She looked at him quizzically. He repeated, "Trust me. It's okay." First came Shadow, then Monster, followed by Gus, Red Velvet, Snowflake, and of course, Speckles. Each creature approached Dolby first and nuzzled his hand with its nose. Each did the same to Hope, who just followed Dolby's lead and did what he did. Only, she did it with her eyes so wide open that they hurt. Three dozen other whitetail and blacktail watched from the border of the clearing. They proceeded to spend the next hour or so together competing in the most bizarre Olympic games that she had ever seen. Hope had been an athlete her whole life, but had never played anything quite like this. She raced Dolby on deerback. They squared off on a joust. She tried to fell a tree with an ax faster than Red Velvet could with his rack. She knocked Dolby off of Monster Horn before he could knock her off of Shadow Muzzle. She even participated in a tug-of-war but knew she didn't contribute much. The entire time she watched her new friend talking and listening and laughing with another species. She had a hunch that something was different about Dolby. She had a gut feeling that it had something to do with wildlife. But she never dreamed that there was such a thing as a half-tail, and that one of her schoolmates—Dolby Hart of all people— was actually one. It was now 4:30 p.m. He had time to tell her a little more of the story, but the whole saga would have to wait. For now, Hope understood that she just got herself mixed up in something that held promise to be either dangerous or heroic, or maybe even both.

21

CLASH

"If a kingdom is divided against itself, that kingdom cannot stand.
If a house is divided against itself, that house cannot stand."

—JESUS IN MARK 3:24

Hope led the way to the Hideaway's office. Two waves of creatures followed—three adolescents first, and then five deer trailing along the treeline. Hope thought Peev wanted her to bring four-legged friends, but she couldn't be sure, so they played it safe and kept the deer hidden. Peev opened the door, said "Hello," and looked around to see if there were others behind them. He walked to the back of the office, opened two slats of the blinds and looked out toward the trees. "Where are the others?" he asked matter-of-factly.

"The others?" Dolby played dumb.

"You know who I mean—your friends."

"These are my friends."

"The ones with tails."

Dolby answered, "How do you know about those friends?"

Peev smiled. "You know who my father is, right?" The kids shook their heads acknowledging that Barney Vanderflunder was his dad. "You know who his best friends are, right?" They admitted that he was very close with the Krantz's. "Well, we know all about her half-tail abilities, and she has filled us in on yours. So, stop playing dumb. I've got something you and

82

your forest friends are going to want to see. I'm trying to help you out here." Dolby looked at Hope who nodded as if to say he could trust Peev.

"I will make sure they follow wherever you take us."

"Good. Let's go then." Peev led them to the garage and onto a cramped golf cart.

Steele took one look at the Chevelle and asked, "Whoa! Can't we take that instead?"

"You like that, huh? It's not something I drive around much anymore." After a short distance, Peev steered the battery-powered vehicle down the long driveway that led to Veep's house. "I'm about to show you something that not many people have seen. Then you can see for yourselves what kind of an uncle you actually have. They are away for the weekend at some awards banquet in Ann Arbor. Understand, he doesn't want people to see this. By this time, Gus, Shadow, Red, Monster, and Snowflake all trotted alongside the vehicle like secret servicemen guarding a presidential motorcade. He punched in a code that unlocked the front door, and they crowded into the entrance of a log cabin the size of a mansion. "It's this way." In a single file line, they walked down a long hallway that was covered with pictures of Veep posing with local dignitaries and big shots. One picture caught Adele's eye. With big eyes, she quietly pointed at a photo of two tuxedo-clad men smiling arm-in-arm. Steele and Dolby recognized the man next to Veep—the warden of Gomer jail. Peev's tour came to a dead-end in a large office. "This is what we in his family call his *secret lair*." He pulled a book toward him from the bookshelf, activating it to open and reveal something very upsetting. "It's important that you see what my brother really thinks of the deer species." They all stepped into a gigantic room. They then pushed forward into the room to be sure they were really seeing what they were seeing. Besides theatre seating aimed at a massive TV, the entire rest of the 1000 square-foot room was filled with full-size stuffed deer, elk, moose, gazelles, and caribou. Along the walls, making a complete square, were mounted heads and antlers of all kinds of members of the deer family. At the sight, something like a gasp came from the mouth of every creature in the room besides Peev. The knees of the deer in the room all buckled. "Sorry to have to show you this but Veep killed every one of these . . ." Peev didn't finish his sentence. A massive set of horns were now lowered and charging right at him. Peev threw his hands up. "I didn't do this! I didn't do this! It wasn't me!" Monster Horn didn't care. How dare he show them this room of death for so many of his kind. Shadow Muzzle jumped in front of the little man and a crash of horns echoed throughout the room. Two sets of antlers locked together as almost half of a ton of deer pushed and shoved back and forth in the middle of the room.

Over the screams and yells of "NO!" Dolby could only make out a few words of what was said during the fight. He heard Monster say, "Get out way—no-tail must pay." Shadow said at one point in a strained voice, "It's not our way. Also, different no-tail did this."

"But he showed to us. Why show us? Are you on side of no-tail?"

Even though Shadow was just about half the weight of Monster Horn, he held his own out of sheer determination. The fight continued with loud clashes and groans for a full two minutes until finally a glass case containing deer pelts smashed into pieces. This was enough to stop the two males from continuing their dual. Dolby had been yelling for them to stop, but they either hadn't heard or hadn't cared. It was now quiet enough to be heard. "STOP! Look what you've done. Veep is going to kill us."

By this time, Peev was cowering in the corner. "I'm sorry. I didn't think this through. I shouldn't have brought you here." Monster Horn made a move toward Peev again but was again intercepted by Shadow Muzzle; this time without a collision.

"Monster! Time for you to cool down. Go!" Despite his rage, the enormous elk obeyed the Half-tail, but did so by diving through the sliding glass window with a crash. "It's time for all of us to leave." They all turned to leave, but in a way that Dolby had not anticipated. Red Velvet and Gus exited the way Monster Horn did with a leap through broken glass. Snowflake stayed with Shadow Muzzle and Dolby. It was a subtle parting of the ways for two groups of deer in Gomer. Nobody could have anticipated that it would be the beginning of a major rift between two deer factions. Each deer in Gomer would soon be forced to pick a side. Some followed Shadow who remained committed to Dolby, their Half-tail. Others aligned themselves with Monster Horn who had it in his mind to take the fight to the no-tails before they could take the fight to them.

"Let's hope Veep sees all the deer fur and concludes that a buck accidentally jumped through his door and did this damage," said Peev. For the first time, the kids noticed that Speckles had not made the trip, which was unlike him.

On their way back, Hope asked Peev a question. "Why are you trying to expose your brother, anyway?"

"Technically, he hasn't been my brother for a long time. He wants nothing to do with me. Besides, I'm tired of how he treats his wife, stepson, and rest of the family. He's really not who you think he is. He's been walking all over us for most of his life. Serves him right if he gets caught."

"Gets caught doing what?" asked Steele.

"I can't be sure, but I think he's up to something that involves Edith. He has visited her a lot at the jail, and as you can see, he really has it in for deer."

Dolby thought about that for a second. "You know, he was acting kinda weird on the fire truck. He made sure I sat in the captain's chair, and then hounded me with questions about being a Half-tail the whole time. It was the first time I ever really felt uncomfortable with him."

Even though he was added to the bottom of the list, Veep had now leapfrogged Peev and everyone else to the top of Dolby's suspicions.

Suspects	Reasons for suspicions	Possible motive
1. Enid Schwartz—lunch lady	—always rude 2 me —serves food so bad could be poison	—???
2. Mildred Snodgrass—librarian	—rude 2 me	—???
3. Jed Calhoun—Turkey-town Owner	—big deer hunter	—suspects Steele involved in the killing of his turkeys
4. Chief Kowalski—police chief	—rude 2 me —reputation 4 being corrupt	—???
5. ~~Percy V. (Peev)—camp-ground manager~~	~~—rude 2 me~~ ~~—creepy, big hunter~~	~~—2 seek revenge 4 Edith while she's in jail?~~
6. Bones—night watchman	—rude 2 me —creepy	—???
7. Miss Daken—6th grade teacher	—nobody is that nice	
8. ~~Barney Vanderflunder—middle school principal~~	~~—multiple visits to Edith Krantz~~	~~—2 seek revenge 4 Edith while she's in jail?~~
9. Perry V. (Veep)—Ranch manager	—big hunter —multiple visits to E. Krantz	—2 seek revenge 4 Edith while she's in jail?

22

GUNSHOT

"Sometimes the man who looks happiest in town, with the biggest smile,
is the one carrying the biggest load of sin . . . half the time he's covering up . . .
On the other hand, the unhappy, pale, put-upon man walking by,
who looks all guilt and sin, why, often that's your good man with a capital G."

—RAY BRADBURY
IN *SOMETHING WICKED THIS WAY COMES* (1962)

SUNDAY

It was well past midnight and there was no settling down for the two girls and two boys sitting around the dying campfire. They were still reeling from the news that Veep—Uncle Veep, of all people—could be Edith Krantz's pawn; a pawn to carry out revenge on Gomer's deer for taking her son so many years ago. They all stared quietly at the fire as if it had hypnotic power over them. Hope broke the trance. "What should we do?"

"About Veep? I've been asking myself that all night," replied Dolby.

"No. I'm sick of thinking about that. What should we do tonight—I'm bored."

Steele spoke up. "I know!"

"Of course, you do," said Adele. "You always have ideas—and they don't always turn out to be good ones."

Steele ignored her. "Let's go bear watching! I haven't done that in forever."

Dolby sighed. "What are you even talking about?"

"Let's go to the dump! This is prime feeding time." Steele had been to the dump numerous times, but there had never been a bear-sighting. He wasn't about to tell them that, though. In relation to the Hideaway campground and the Gomer Ranch, the dump, of course, was located closest to the Hideaway. In fact, on some nights, depending on how the wind blew, one could smell garbage far better than campfire smoke or burgers on a grill. "It's literally a ten-minute bike ride. It'll be awesome! Let's go."

"Why do I let myself get talked into this stuff? There's no way this ends well," predicted Adele. "There aren't even bears around here, are there?" Adele was attaching the leash to Zeke just in case.

"I guess you'll see!" Steele teased. Normally up for an adventure, Dolby was adventured-out. But Steele was as persuasive as ever.

They hid their bikes in a nearby ditch at the front gate of the dumping ground. Steele had clearly done this before. He easily found the part of the fence that could be squeezed through. Instantly, they gagged from the stench. "Yep. Smells like garbage," said Hope. "This place has really gone to the dumps."

"Sssshhhh," came the reply from the other three. They followed a road through the middle of the dump and could already hear odd night sounds surrounding them. Steele had planned on scaring the girls, until he found himself too scared to carry out the plan. He had instructed his friends not to turn on their flashlights until the opportune time. Satisfied with their location, Steele stopped.

"Listen!"

They all concentrated on the night sounds. Besides the sound of Zeke's low growl, there was movement and rummaging around them. They heard the yelping of a pack of coyote who seemed to be attacking who knows what. There were leaves and tree noises coming from the surrounding woods. And, of course, there were the familiar songs of crickets and frogs, and the chittering of raccoons. The previous times Steele had gone to the dump, they would turn on their flashlights at the same time in order to watch the animals scurry. He was about to yell, "Now!" but this time, never got to that point. From the dump's office to their left, a noise interrupted his plan. It was obviously a human voice, but he or she made no human sound. What could be best described as a chirping or chattering noise echoed through the dump. Thanks to the light of a full moon, the kids could see what seemed like hundreds of raccoons stop their dining and race toward the noise. At this, the kids knew that it was time to go. They, themselves, raced back toward their bikes. Once they peddled out of earshot, Dolby was the first to speak.

"There are plenty of things that confuse me—but what just happened was not one of them. I have witnessed something like that before; so have you Steele. Remember when the treehouse was on fire and the Pitcoywolves were fighting our deer friends?"

"That's right," remembered Steele. "Old fart Krantz yelled in a wolf language for them to return."

"We just saw something similar. I am confident that those raccoons were being called by a raccoon half-tail. What other explanation is there? Raccoons don't typically behave that way."

"Do you think it is somebody we know?" asked Hope.

"I wouldn't be surprised," answered Dolby. "Maybe Geema can help us with this one?"

The next morning, they awoke early to check out the area around the dump for more clues before church. They never made it to the front gate. Halfway there, they recognized Uncle Veep's green SUV pulled over to the side of the road. They ditched their bikes and sneaked ninja-style through the woods. They saw something in a clearing that made them stop in their tracks. A good-looking, salt-and-pepper-haired man pointed a pistol at point-blank range toward a helpless deer who looked back at him with pleading eyes. Dolby recognized Princess, a female that he knew from the first day he met Snowflake. Dolby wanted to cry out but knew that he couldn't. Adele turned away just in time. Steele, Hope, and Dolby weren't so lucky. With a quick pull of the trigger, they watched the body of Princess lurch back in response to the strike of a bullet. But Princess was not dead. She dragged her body away from the killer, but was too slow. He took two more steps toward her, pulled the trigger once more, and landed a fatal blow to the back of her head. Dolby fought back tears as he watched Princess collapse in a heap to the ground. Veep calmly placed the smoking gun in its holder and coldly walked back to his car. They all sank to their knees both out of horror and to avoid being spotted. Dolby didn't know what to do, so he did what always seemed to make sense. He blew his whistle.

23

RACCOONS

"You be careful. People in masks cannot be trusted."

—WILLIAM GOLDMAN IN *THE PRINCESS BRIDE* (1973)

Since yesterday's fight, Dolby hadn't seen any of his deer friends, not even Snowflake or Monster who left soon after Shadow, Red, and Gus. He checked his watch. Adele finally spoke up. "We can't wait any longer, my parents are waiting for us to go to church. It's been an hour, Dolby."

"But I just don't understand. This has never happened before. Why aren't they responding to my whistle?"

"I wonder if it has something to do with yesterday's disagreement?" Hope added.

"Maybe," said a perplexed boy, "but they always come." Dolby felt vulnerable all of a sudden. He remembered when Red Velvet said something to the effect of, *this better be good or else the next time you blow that thing, we might not show up.* He realized that he just went from the boy who talked to deer to the boy who cried wolf. The thought sickened him almost as much as seeing the buzzards circling above Princess's lifeless body.

He had forgotten the details of the story, so when he got back home, he asked Geema about *The Boy Who Cried Wolf.* She was spending the day canning strawberry jams and jellies, so she had all the time in the world to tell stories. "Ah, yes. The boy who cried wolf. Told that one to your mother many times. It's about a shepherd boy who tricks nearby villagers into thinking that a wolf was attacking the town's flock. He tricks them over and over again until they don't believe him when a wolf actually shows up. When he calls for help for real, nobody comes, and the sheep are eaten by the wolf." Dolby winced at the way Geema ended the story. He desperately hoped his story wouldn't end that way for him, with his flock of deer being destroyed by a wolf or something due to his crying wolf too much. He quickly changed the subject.

Meanwhile, the first thing Steele did when he got home was to take a bike ride with Adele to the treehouse. They were impressed with how much Dolby had cleaned up and fixed, which made their search a little more challenging. After a thorough look at the inside, nothing was discovered. There were also no clues on the wrap-around deck.

"Nothing over here, either." Adele had checked out the suspension bridge and second sitting area. She used the zip-line to get down while Steele took the stairs.

"There's got to be something," exclaimed Steele. As they examined the ground surrounding the tree fort, clues finally began to emerge. "Look at this! Yep—they are all over." Steele used a stick to point out small hand-shaped tracks in the mud. "See . . . five finger-like toes on all of these."

"Raccoons!" said Adele. "Just as we suspected."

"Ew! And lots of raccoon evidence over here too." He pointed to piles of droppings. "See, they are small and cylinder-shaped."

"And—gross!—full of berries."

"Geema?"

"Yes dear?" She handed him a strawberry covered in sugar.

"Great-Great-Grandpa Clarence was a fox half-tail, right?"

"Mmm-hmmmm," she replied with her own mouth full of strawberry.

"Mom is a fox half-tail. I'm a deer half-tail."

"What's your question, sweetie?"

"Have you ever heard of a raccoon half-tail?"

She put down the potato masher she was using to smush the berries. "That's a good question. I can't say that I've heard of one. Not likely, in my mind."

"Why do you say that?"

"Well, for one, raccoons are good for nothin'. What use would they be to anybody? All they do is rummage through garbage. I don't see it, personally. Although . . ." Dolby waited. "They can do a lot with those little hands'a theirs. I've seen 'em open up doors, cabinets, latches, even bottles. They can also climb like a cat on a scratchin' post. I changed my mind. Maybe it is possible after all. What makes you ask such a thing?"

"No reason. Just wondering."

"Dolby Brad Hart," she slammed a bowl down on the counter. "What. Makes. You. Ask?" Dolby caved and told her everything. By now the strawberry mixture was boiling on the stove. "Now you be careful, young man. Anyone who is a half-tail to raccoons is nobody you want to be messin' with. Raccoons have always reminded me of evil and darkness. Maybe 'cause they are nocturnal and always prowlin' around at night." She pointed her spatula at him. "You know nothin' good ever happens after midnight."

"Yes ma'am."

"That reminds me of something else. I wonder if I still have that somewhere. Here—keep stirring." Geema slowly climbed the wooden steps to the attic. She couldn't tell which creaked more—the stairs or her knees. Dolby heard rummaging around up there for a while until he heard the words, "Aha!" She returned with a framed poem. "This was actually written by your Great-Great Grampa Clarence. He wrote it as if the raccoon represented his sin and temptations. It's kinda weird but makes some sense somehow. I want you to have it. Maybe it'll serve as a warning to you to be careful with both raccoons and the sins and struggles you will face. You don't have to read it now but give it some thought later."

"Thanks, Geema." Dolby took it up to his room. Later that night, he hopped into bed and read the following:

The Raccoon
Clarence Withers III

You look so harmless . . . so innocent.
The longer I look, the more harmless you seem.
The longer I look, the more attracted I become.

A Half-Tail Uprising

It's *just* a raccoon . . . *only* a raccoon.

You look so good . . . but that mask
What's behind the mask?

When far in the distance, you seem invisible.
But then that hideous call comes;
A chittering that makes me shudder.
What's behind that hideous call?

But then you come,
Sneaking around like a coward.
At night you come,
Surrounded by the darkness.
Alone you come,
Sneaking around like a coward.

You hide in the brush just waiting to pounce.
Waiting. Waiting. Waiting.

Don't you know how much destruction you cause?
Don't you see how much destruction he will cause?

The mask.
The call.
Hiding something. Hiding something.

But then light.
The sun rises, and you hastily scamper away.
It's morning, and I now see clearly.
You're not lovely after all.
You're a bandit, a pillager, a pirate.
Your whole reason for living is to destroy . . . to rob.
You're a *robber* . . . come to rob me of *everything*.

24

SIMILARITIES

"He always had a droll way of drawing striking comparisons between savage animals and civilized men that showed a considerable knowledge of the former, and a keen, though somewhat cynical, estimate of the latter."

—EDGAR RICE BURROUGHS
IN *THE RETURN OF TARZAN* (1913)

There were two places that Dolby retreated to when feeling down, abandoned, confused, bored, or just simply with the need to think. One was the treehouse, and the second was the wooden shed filled with fireworks that Swampy Canis had built for him in the empty field near Hart Castle. Shooting off fireworks had a cathartic effect for Dolby; it relieved stress; it helped him think. It gave him a feeling of power when he had none. It made him feel in control when life was otherwise unraveling. The only time he hesitated to shoot off pyrotechnics was when he wanted to talk to his deer friends. They would stay away for obvious reasons when he was having his own personal fourth of July. On this day, he didn't care that he was chasing off the whitetail. He didn't want them there anyway after they abandoned him and his whistle upon the death of Princess. He thought about the possibility that the deer were no longer his friends and lit a fuse. BOOM! A Cherry Bomb exploded. He thought about the new faction that had been created between the two groups of deer, which could make them vulnerable in the case of an attack. BAM! An M-80 blasted his eardrums. He thought about Veep murdering Princess in cold blood. POP-POP-POP-POP-POP! He lit a string of Thunderbomb firecrackers. Who needs a professional counselor, he thought? These firecrackers were doing the trick. After lighting off a few Roman Candles, Dolby caught movement in the woods beyond the fence. He walked over to find Snowflake alone. "Are you quite done with those fireworkers?"

"You know they're called fireworks."

"Not to me! They start fires and they scare me."

"Well, you're scaring me," Dolby retorted. "Where have you been?"

"I have bad news."

"Okay."

"Princess died yesterday. The whitetail have been away in mourning."

"I know. I was there and actually saw it. I still can't believe Uncle Veep could be so evil. And I can't believe you didn't come when I whistled." Dolby was too hurt to put himself in anyone else's shoes, or hooves for that matter.

"First of all, we couldn't come. There was still thunderstick powder in the air. Whitetail protocol prevents us from moving in the direction of thunderstick. We are instructed to stay away. We knew you were okay so there was no need to answer your call. Secondly, as you know, there is widespread division among us. To be honest, each side didn't want to come in case the other side showed up. Shoot, I haven't even seen Speckles in a week or more. Thirdly, nobody wanted to see the accident scene or Princess like that."

"Accident scene? What do you mean—what I saw was no accident."

"You saw what happened before the no-tail arrived?"

"No. He was already there when we first saw him," Dolby replied.

"Then you missed the accident."

"What accident?" Dolby was getting impatient.

"In the early morning fog, Princess jumped in front of a moving . . . what do you call it? Um . . . car. The no-tail ran right into Princess. She had broken both back legs and was tossed over a ditch. But, instead of checking on her, the no-tail left the scene like a coward."

"So, Veep wasn't even the one to hit her?"

"No," answered Snowflake with voice shaking. "He came later and discovered a bloody Princess in a ton of pain. He did what I think you would call the humane thing to do—he ended her life, and he did it quickly to put a stop to her suffering and pain. She was surely going to die right where she laid anyway."

"So, Veep was trying to do what was right?"

"We believe so—everything seems to indicate that."

"Wow. I am so confused. Does that mean he's not the raccoon half-tail, then? If not, then who is?"

Back at the 150-year-old farmhouse, four teenagers filled Geema in on how the weekend went over iced tea and lemonade. She sensed that there was more they wanted to say, so she stayed put on the front porch. The friends alternated between playing on the tire swing hanging from the cherry tree and throwing a frisbee back and forth. All of the whispering and nodding and gesturing didn't keep Geema from nodding off in her rocking chair, though. She awoke to the four of them rocking beside her. With a stretch and a yawn, she giggled, "Go ahead . . . out with it you four!"

They looked at one another and Dolby dragged his rocker closer. "Can you tell us . . . is there a way to tell if someone is a half-tail?"

"Still searchin', eh?" They expected the answer to be something like either "no, it's impossible to tell," or, something spiritual like, "Only God above can reveal that to a body." What they got instead was a very simple, practical answer. "Oh honeys, that's an easy one. But first you have to know what animal they are able to communicate with. If you don't have that, then it's right difficult."

"So, you're saying that once you know what animal they are connected with, then it's easy to figure out?"

"Exactly."

"How so?" chimed in Adele. Hope remained silent since she felt like she had entered another universe with all this stuff. Steele was silent because he felt sick from eating too many cherries.

"You see, in my experience, half-tails almost always have similar characteristics as the species they can understand. That's partly why it's so easy for them to communicate and comprehend—in a way, you can say it's like they are one with that animal. All you have to do is study that particular animal, and then study any suspected humans, and it should lead you right to him or her. For example, first watch the fox; get to know the fox; then look at your mom and you'll see what I mean."

"Okay, lemme try." Dolby was more excited at this assignment than any he'd ever had in school. "Foxes are beautiful animals, intelligent, sneaky, mysterious, and independent."

"What else?" asked Geema who was enjoying playing the teacher.

"They are not pack animals—they live in small families. They are also loyal and good caretakers of their children."

"So, who does that sound like?"

Dolby shook his head. "Mom! . . . That's totally Mom. But foxes are also very playful. Mom is not like that very often, though."

"True," the instructor admitted. "It's not fail-safe. Not every characteristic is found in the human. But in general, the half-tail is a lot like its tailed critter counterpart."

"My turn," Adele said with eyebrows raised. "I'll do Dolby!"

"Oh boy." Dolby did not like the sound of that.

"Okay, deer are usually cautious, easily spooked, curious, playful, and graceful."

"That's Dolby all right—except for the graceful part!" Steele suddenly felt a little better. "Oh, and don't forget one more thing." Dolby was afraid to ask. "When he's talking with girls, he freezes like a deer caught in the headlights!" Dolby groaned and quickly changed the subject.

"So, who matches a raccoon? If we figure that out, we may find our enemy."

At the treehouse, Dolby edited his list once again. This time, the only progress was that Veep was crossed off of consideration. If Snowflake trusted Veep, then it was good enough for Dolby.

Suspects	Reasons for suspicions	Possible motive
1. Enid Schwartz—lunch lady	—always rude 2 me —serves food so bad could be poison	—???
2. Mildred Snodgrass—librarian	—rude 2 me	—???
3. Jed Calhoun—Turkeytown Owner	—big deer hunter	—suspects Steele involved in the killing of his turkeys
4. Chief Kowalski—police chief	—rude 2 me —reputation 4 being corrupt	—???
5. ~~Percy V. (Peev)—campground manager~~	~~—rude 2 me~~ ~~—creepy, big hunter~~	~~—2 seek revenge 4 Edith while she's in jail?~~
6. Bones—night watchman	—rude 2 me —creepy	—???
7. Miss Daken—6th grade teacher	—nobody is that nice	
8. ~~Barney Vanderflunder—middle school principal~~	~~—multiple visits to Edith Krantz~~	~~—2 seek revenge 4 Edith while she's in jail?~~
9. ~~Perry V. (Veep)—Ranch manager~~	~~—big hunter~~ ~~—multiple visits to E. Krantz~~	~~—2 seek revenge 4 Edith while she's in jail?~~

25

BONES

"But even now there is hope left . . . But this I will say to you:
your Quest stands upon the edge of a knife. Stray but a little and it will fail,
to the ruin of all. Yet hope remains while all the Company is true."

—J.R.R. TOLKIEN IN *THE LORD OF THE RINGS:
THE FELLOWSHIP OF THE RING* (1954)

It was too late to meet up at the Dew Drop Inn headquarters, so they
took to the treehouse instead. It was also too late to go out of their way
to fetch some free expired snacks. This, of course, made their craving for
Frito-Lay all the more powerful. "So, let's make a list. When you think of a
raccoon, what characteristics do you picture?" Dolby had pen and journal
in hand, but wished he was in front of the whiteboard. Random qualities
and features were yelled out one right after the other.

"Nocturnal."

"Sneaky."

"Dirty."

"Scavengers."

"Bold."

"Creepy."

"Active."

"Destructive."

"Also, unpredictable."

After a few moments of awkward silence, Dolby held up the note-pad. "Okay, who most closely matches these characteristics? Lunch lady Schwartz?"

"Maybe," came one reply.

"What about librarian Snodgrass?"

"I don't know. Not really?"

"How about Jed Calhoun?"

"Not at all," stated Steele. Everyone agreed. At least they had probably narrowed it down by one.

"Chief Kowalski?"

"Oooh. That's a big fat maybe." Hope finally spoke up, feeling more comfortable with it all.

"Okay. We'll add a question mark next to Kowalski. What about . . ."

"BONES!" interrupted Adele. "Think about it—Bones is always up at night, kinda creepy and dirty, and is always sneaking up on you."

"I'd say unpredictable too," said Dolby. "Definitely someone to keep our eye on. Miss Daken?"

"Please. Of course not."

"Wait, back to Bones." Dolby's mind was racing now. "He always has dark bags under his eyes, just like a raccoon! Plus, he's always eating like a scavenger. Besides the fact that most of the time I've seen raccoons, he hasn't been too far behind."

"You know what else?" Hope asked. "Now that I think about it, my Mom once told me that he was Uncle Veep's stepson. Which means . . ."

"Nooooo. Are you kidding me? He's a Vanderflunder too?!" Dolby exclaimed. "He could totally be the one planning with Mrs. Krantz."

Adele agreed. "Looks like we may have found our guy."

Steele jumped in. "Man, is everybody a Vanderflunder in this town?"

Adele laughed and said, "It *is* Gomer. Everybody is related to each other somehow!"

"So, what do we do now?" Hope asked, assuming that the veteran detectives would have a plan.

All three shook their heads. Adele spoke for them all— "I really have no idea."

The rest of the summer flew by, as it always does. Nothing of real consequence happened in the lives of the Gomer friends, unless you include the time they were baling hay at the Brown's farm and Dolby left the gate to the horse pen open. Adele and her parents spent the better part of the day tracking down fourteen horses enjoying a rare summer day of freedom in rural Gomer. Dolby spent that day kicking himself for being so stupid. Adele told him later about a related weird horse fact. If they would have been able to keep just one horse from escaping the fenced-in area, the rest of the horses would have stayed close by together and not run off, even though they were free of the pen. But, the second all of them were free, they felt the freedom to run wherever they wanted.

As for the deer, they were always around. But, Dolby's relationship with them had grown cold—maybe a sign that the honeymoon had ended for the Half-tail and his former close friends. Dolby often wondered if what drove the final wedge between them was his constant cry for help. He also wondered if the deer of Gomer had more important things to tend to, like trying to get along.

When school started, the four friends spent little time together. This was no fault of their own. It's just what happens when one enters high school, one begins eighth grade and is busy with soccer, and two start seventh grade with few classes together. Combine all of the other factors—family, homework, chores, other extra-curricular activities—and it's a recipe for drifting apart. That's why, when Gomer Middle School announced that the seventh-grade trip was back on after a three-year hiatus, Dolby was excited to reconnect with Adele and Hope. Most years, the eighth-grade class took an end-of-the-year trip to Washington D.C. and the seventh graders spent three days and two nights at Gomer Ranch for a team-building retreat. It was Mr. Vanderflunder's idea years ago in response to the growing problem with bullying that every middle school seems to have to tackle. Ironically, money in the school budget had dried up and there was no funding for anything extra when the bullying was at its worst over the past three years.

Steele maintains that had nothing to do with him. It was merely coincidence that the worst three years just happened to be the three years he spent at Gomer Middle School. The elderly principal had four years to prepare for the upcoming camp, so both students and teachers were excited to see what Barney had up his sleeve. He may have been old and out-of-touch, but he was also full of creative ideas to bring unity and promote cooperation when there was none.

Dolby and Hope were texting about what to bring, what to wear, and what kinds of activities they might be doing. Hope had secretly applied to be a junior chaperone—an honor given to eighth graders who demonstrate leadership potential—and in the end, was an honor given to Hope. She had to do some serious bargaining with her parents because going on the three-day trip meant missing two soccer practices. Hope was able to persuade her parents with the same quick thinking she used to convince Peev she was a college student. "It'll look good on a resume," "I'll be learning leadership skills," and "It may help me get an athletic scholarship," were among her arguments.

On the eve of something exciting like Christmas morning or a camping trip, sleep often eluded Dolby. The same was true on this night, but for additional reasons. He would be going back to where Bones lived and worked; back to where raccoons reigned; back to being in potential danger again. This time, though, he would be going back without the aid of many of his friends which included Steele, and those of the hooved variety. He must've nodded off, though, because he was startled awake by the breath of somebody standing over him. "Ah! Stop doing that!" It was Snowflake who came and went at the farmhouse as she pleased—sometimes even in the middle of the night. "What time is it?" The digital clock next to his bed read 2:30 a.m.

"You have visitors," was all that Snowflake said before she click-clacked carefully down the wooden stairs. Dolby threw on a t-shirt and flip-flops and stumbled downstairs and out the sliding glass door. Waiting to meet him behind the house were the same five Sitka messenger deer that delivered the first message. The reddish-brown creatures lowered their heads upon the Half-tail's arrival.

Without realizing it, Dolby transformed into the great Half-tail. "Chinook, Panuk, Qannik, Nanook, and Suka. Greetings." How did he remember their names? They all bowed once again.

"We bring word again from Fantasma the Wise." Dolby hoped it was more than just one word this time. It wasn't. "The message is . . . *Rescue*."

"The message is rescue?" asked Dolby.

"Rescue."

Dolby had barely put the two messages together in his mind before *The Albino Express* had saluted, turned as one, and bounced away.

"*Search* and *rescue*. *Search and rescue*. I wish Fantasma would be clearer," said Dolby to Snowflake. "But if I had to guess, she is preparing me to head up a rescue of some kind." He didn't yet understand the messages, but he understood the timing of them. The next day's camping trip to Gomer Ranch was not going to be an ordinary one. That he knew for sure.

Only two words (or is it one?) were added to Dolby's journal. But they were enough to possibly solve the mystery. *Raccoon-like* was now listed as a reason to suspect Bones. No motive was determined yet, however.

Suspects	Reasons for suspicions	Possible motive
1. Enid Schwartz—lunch lady	—always rude 2 me —serves food so bad could be poison	—???
2. Mildred Snodgrass—librarian	—rude 2 me	—???
3. Jed Calhoun—Turkey-town owner	—big deer hunter	—???
4. Chief Kowalski—police chief	—rude 2 me —reputation 4 being corrupt	—???
5. ~~Percy V. (Peev)—campground manager~~	~~—rude 2 me~~ ~~—creepy, big hunter~~	~~—2 seek revenge 4 Edith while she's in jail?~~
6. Bones—night watchman	—rude 2 me —creepy, raccoon-like	—???
7. Miss Daken—6th grade teacher	—nobody is that nice	
8. ~~Barney Vanderflunder—middle school principal~~	~~—multiple visits to Edith Krantz~~	~~—2 seek revenge 4 Edith while she's in jail?~~
9. ~~Perry V. (Veep)—Ranch manager~~	~~—big hunter~~ ~~—multiple visits to E. Krantz~~	~~—2 seek revenge 4 Edith while she's in jail?~~

26

EXPLOSION

"A man's life is like a walk down a passage lined with closed windows. As you reach each window, an unknown hand opens it and the light it lets in only increases by contrast the darkness of the end of the passage."

—WINSTON CHURCHILL (1941)

TUESDAY, 9:00 a.m.

Dolby, Adele, and Hope sat together as the school bus tossed kids around like some kind of lame roller coaster. Dolby was lost in thought as the bus carrying rowdy seventh graders cut through the birch tree-lined entrance to what looked more like a resort than a camp and conference center. The stress of the trip had clearly caught up with him, because he couldn't decide if the waving branches from the rows of trees were welcoming him or trying to shoo him away. At the same time as their arrival, another very different group was arriving at a very different kind of camp. Armies of foreign deer species were settling into the old base headquarters like troops readying for battle. Lunch lady Enid was the first to greet the students. She climbed the steps of the bus and asked if there were any dietary needs. One girl sheepishly raised her hand and announced that she was lactose intolerant, gluten-free, and a vegetarian. Clearly annoyed, Enid mumbled to herself, "All right, then, I guess you'll be eating sweet potatoes and eggs for every meal." The first thing teachers did as students filed off of the two buses was to collect their cell phones. Mr. V's theory was that in order to get the most out of the unity-building few days, contact with the outside world would be counter-productive. Mr. Vanderflunder was sincere in his desire to see his students build relationships with each other rather than seeing them tear one another apart. He was also very sincere in his desire to preserve his own sanity and make his job easier with less disciplinary issues. The morning was spent getting settled into cabins, going over rules, playing some get-to-know-you type games, and lunch. It didn't escape Dolby's attention that many familiar faces were helping run the camp—Peev, Bones, Lunch Lady Schwartz, and of course, the ringleader of the three days—Uncle Veep. Each lunch table had to send a volunteer to gather the table scraps and scrape them into a composting barrel out back. Of course, Dolby was voluntold by his table. After dumping his garbage, he watched as Enid Schwartz carried, and then dumped, leftover deviled eggs and Sloppy Joe meat into the nearest bushes. Was she leaving the leftover food for the raccoons? Dolby made a mental note.

1:00 p.m.

After lunch, it was time to get organized at the Welcome Center. Approximately seventy-five students and fifteen teachers and staff were divided into three different groups for the retreat's afternoon activities. Dolby and Adele were separated into different teams, and Hope was helping with the other group. Dolby and his twenty-five students were assigned first to horseback riding. Adele and the second similar-sized bunch headed toward a paintball field nestled in a valley. Hope's third cluster ascended a hill toward an open, level, playing area. Each group made their way in silence due to the uncomfortable relationships purposely put together by Mr. V. Their return trip from the afternoon's adventures, however, would not be so quiet. The gang on the hill was introduced to a new spin on the traditional Capture the Flag game. As an alternative to the standard method of play—winning by finding, securing, and then returning the opponent's flag to one's side—a wooden apparatus was placed at each end of the football field-sized area. Each gadget held an upright two-liter bottle of Diet Coke along with an attached sleeve of Mentos candies. When a corresponding string was pulled, the candies would tumble down a plastic chute and plunge into the cola causing a volcanic eruption of stickiness. The resulting fizzy fountain then served as foaming feedback to all that the game had been won. But despite this fun new twist, it didn't keep another twisted turn of events from following. After thirty minutes of the novelty not wearing off in the least, a sweaty, sporty, Hope sprinted past a colony of defenders who were distracted by other opponents. She weaved her way through the second swarm of defense. Although mostly in the clear, she had only the star quarterback to beat. He lunged out his arm to tag her. She dove for the string. Her first attempt failed as she landed headfirst at the base of the cola contraption. She rolled over just in time to yank the rope before the boy landed at her feet. He fell hard on his oft-injured shoulder, dislocating it once again, and yelled in pain. She lay there for a few seconds anticipating the cascade of Coke like a winning coach bracing for a Gatorade bath. But the geyser never gushed. Feeling both a sense of relief and disappointment, there was no time to delay. Hope's teammates awaited her celebration. She danced away toward them. But then came the explosion. Only this one wasn't carbonation. This was *detonation*. When she pulled the cord, it triggered something drastically more violent than a soda pop shower. Chaos ensued. Children recoiled and shrieked and scattered. Teachers frantically corralled crying kids and followed two camp staffers back down toward the Welcome Center to safety. Minutes before, Mr. Vanderflunder had been enjoying both the reprieve from the kids and the peaceful stroll around the lake as he himself headed back toward the welcome building. He checked his watch. Things seemed to be going according to plan. The chirping birds around him soothed his anxious thoughts . . . temporarily. It was at that moment that the world of the camp literally exploded with pandemonium. First came the boom that roared and echoed across the valley. The shrieks of birds and flapping of wings followed in unison out of nearby trees. Next came the howling of children. The disturbance was loud enough to spook not only the horses, but also the adolescent horseback riders. Two other camp workers took charge and led the group quickly back to the starting point. Down on the paintball course, the players were panic-stricken mid-game, first by the loud blast, then by a couple of peculiar masked gunmen who themselves violently erupted from the dense brush. Only theirs weren't paintball guns. Their appearance after the bang was clearly no coincidence—the explosion was their cue. The children and teachers were paraded at gunpoint back through the woods toward the front of the camp. It became clear as the entire seventh grade converged together that they were the victims of some kind of a coordinated attack. The thought ran through many of their heads—why would anybody want to hold an entire seventh grade hostage? They were driven to the back wall of the Welcome Center and forced to huddle together in whimpering clumps where they awaited instructions. They didn't have to wait long. The click and whine of a megaphone overpowered their muffled sobs. A male voice trumpeted through the fear. "STOP CRYING AND LISTEN TO ME NOW."

27

INFIRMARY

"Time, with his innumerable horse-power, worked away,
not minding what anybody said."

—CHARLES DICKENS IN *HARD TIMES* (1854)

2:15 p.m.

As the cowering heads of children looked up, the terror on their faces quickly gave way to looks of confusion and betrayal. The voice behind the handheld speaker was a shaky one. It belonged to none other than Principal Vanderflunder! The megaphone continued but with a decidedly defeated tone. "I am sorry for how this has turned out. I did not mean to scare you this badly. This was organized with the camp staff ahead of time and clearly got out of hand fast. I honestly wasn't aware that they were going to use an actual explosive or scare you with fake gunmen." He glared at Peev and Bones who had just removed their ski masks. "Even though they took it too far, it *was* my idea to shake you up a bit. I was just trying to simulate a realistic scenario where you would be forced to work together to resolve some kind of dilemma. Not that it probably matters now . . ." Mr. V. stopped mid-sentence, sighed, but felt the urge to continue in order to defend himself. "But have you heard of Escape Rooms? An Escape Room is an adventure game where players are locked in a room and have to use clues inside to figure out how to escape within a set time limit. This was to be your escape room." Kids shook their heads in disbelief and the teachers, with whom he should have first consulted, glared at him with daggers of fury. "Why don't we all take a breather—we have gotten off to a very bad start. We still have two more days left together so let's try to make the most of this retreat anyway." He gathered the teachers together. After a heart-felt apology, the old man attempted to redeem the rest of their time at the ranch. He was able to ease the tension a little with his last words into the bullhorn. "I guess I really Vanderflundered this one, huh?" Even the fuming teachers couldn't help but chuckle a little at that one.

Meanwhile, deep in the forest, various foreign deer species were on high alert after the sound of the explosion, which announced, like a trumpet call, that war was approaching. Wapiti and Canuck were now there, as were Zayan and Saluja, along with many other Elk, Whitetail, and Moose, some of whom were making their first trip to Gomer.

In another part of the forest, but much closer to Dolby, Steele was still shaking and still hiding after the explosion. His application to be a student chaperone was denied due to certain past failings. But he was very concerned about what the next two days had in store. So, he skipped school and set up a personal headquarters in a small, out-of-the-way cabin that was left vacant. He didn't even need to lie to his dad. It wasn't like he was around much lately anyway. Steele would work in the shadows of the camp, not unlike Shadow Muzzle's role, just in case Dolby needed his help.

3:00 p.m.

Once the dust settled and the students had recovered from their scare, Mr. V. and the teachers returned with a new plan of attack. Each student was given a colored ribbon in order to divide into smaller groups. Teachers held up their team's color as groups began to form and depart to different rooms in the Welcome Center. During the commotion, Dolby did not receive a ribbon. He eventually approached the only adult left in the room to ask what he should do. Veep responded with a big smile, a high-five, and "Oooh. You're the lucky duck! Come with me!" Veep walked him upstairs to the second floor infirmary where nurses bandaged boo-boos, treated poison ivy, and took temperatures. The room was empty except for a rickety, old cot in the corner and a steaming hot pizza on the counter. "This is for you! Dad always does this exercise with students where they have to work together and sort through clues in order to find the missing student. It usually only takes about an hour, but you'll have to be cooped up in here with pop and pizza in the meantime. Are you willing to be the guinea pig?"

Dolby eyed the pizza. As an introvert, he wasn't disappointed to be away from the chaos for a little bit—especially after all the afternoon stress. "Sure. I'll take one for the team," he said with mouth already full of pepperoni. The chewing was so loud he almost missed a familiar beep. Uncle Veep put his phone back into his pocket. "Did you just record that?" Dolby wondered.

"Oh yeah. We always do in case parents get upset. It just shows that you were giving us permission to . . ." Veep chuckled while making air quotes with his fingers, ". . . hold you hostage!" Dolby didn't make much of the statement because he was thinking of a question that he had for Veep.

"So, I saw you shoot the deer on Sunday over the July fourth weekend."

"You saw that, did ya? I hated to do it—very upsetting to me, but I had no choice. That poor doe was dying. I can't believe somebody hit it and didn't stick around." After a few moments of silence, with tears in his eyes, Veep remembered who he was talking to and asked, "Oh, did you know that particular deer?"

Dolby reply came also with glassy eyes. "Yes. That was Princess. I didn't know her as well as some of the others, but she was very close to Snowflake, who I am very tight with."

After another appropriately timed silence, Veep looked at his watch. "Okay, well, enjoy your pizza. I've got some appointments, so I don't think I'll see you until tomorrow. My guess is Peev will be here to relieve you in around forty-five minutes or so, unless a team finds you first! Have fun!"

Dolby had plenty of time to look around the old musty sickroom. Like a guest in the bathroom at a dinner party, the first thing he did was to go through all the cupboards and drawers. He found all kinds of medical treasures like athletic tape, syringes, and Calamine Lotion. There was nothing much to read on the bookshelf except for medical manuals and a dusty Bible. One of the hanging pictures was the Norman Rockwell print that seemed to be in every doctor's office he had ever visited. The boredom began to set in, but at least he wasn't getting a shot in the rear like the boy in the painting.

28

WALDO

"A guy needs somebody—to be near him."
He whined, "A guy goes nuts if he ain't got nobody."

—JOHN STEINBECK IN *OF MICE AND MEN* (1937)

4:15 p.m.

Dolby stared out the window of the infirmary, which faced the rear of the Welcome Center. There wasn't much to look at. Besides a few picnic tables and a grill, there was only about fifty yards of grassy lawn, and acres and acres of corn belonging to a neighboring farmer ready for the September harvest. The cornstalks looked to stand twice his height and almost begged him to run up and down its rows. The leaves on the trees were really starting to change colors—beautiful reds, oranges, and yellows mixed in with the green—but they could only keep his interest for so long. The nearest building was the horse barn to his right. It was too far away to see much of anything, but Dolby knew it well since it was Adele's favorite part of the Ranch. Gomer Stables was known statewide for its massive boarding program, riding trails, and arena. He didn't know how many horses were currently being housed, but with its award-winning retired horse program, there had to be one hundred horses easy. There was little to watch, so Dolby began to play a game of *find the squirrel* or *track a blue jay*. He looked at the wall clock and sighed. Thankfully, the door finally burst open. Peev entered as sweaty and nervous as ever carrying a plate of something chocolate. "So sorry—this is taking longer than expected. You know my dad. He has never been the best at staying on task. The *Where's Dolby?* exercise just got started, so you may be here for another hour yet. This should make up for it, though! It'll tide you over until dinner. Enid is serving it for dessert. I taste-tested it just to be sure it's okay." He smiled and handed him the plate of dirt pudding.

"Ooooh! Worth it!" Dolby exclaimed while grabbing for the treat. "I love the crushed Oreos!" He used a fork to dig around for gummy worms. Finding none, he figured they must be too expensive to include. As he shoveled dirt into his mouth, the idea of eating more food in just an hour wasn't very appealing. An open pizza box revealed that over half of a pie was now missing.

Whether a sugar crash in his bloodstream was to blame, or eating too much and falling into a food coma, or simply from sheer boredom, Dolby fell fast asleep on the otherwise uncomfortable cot.

5:05 p.m.

He awoke with a start as gray hair in a hairnet and bun hovered over him. Lunch lady Enid Schwartz was standing over him yelling in a raspy, smoker's voice, "Where do you want this?"

"Ugh. I don't want that," replied Dolby trying to gather himself from the scare. She was holding a tray with some kind of mystery meat and mashed something. Enid seemed offended, made a humpf sound, and plopped the tray next to the uneaten pizza. Unknown food flew onto the table.

Upon leaving, she yelled as if Dolby was the one hard of hearing, "I was told to bring that. You're welcome."

He checked the time. "5:05 p.m.? It's been two whole hours. This is getting ridiculous." Out of habit, he reached into his pocket for his cell phone to call Adele. Of course, it wasn't there. For the first time, he recalled Uncle Veep's words and wondered if he was, in fact, being held hostage.

Hope and Adele saw each other for the first time since being separated and sat at a corner table. They kept one eye on their food and one on the general dining hall commotion in order to wave Dolby over. They had been busy and therefore thought nothing of the last two hours, assuming Dolby was simply in another room with another group. They began to worry, though, when he never appeared. After talking it over, they decided that there was nobody to ask about his whereabouts since everyone was a suspect. They were also pretty sure none of the other teachers or students were even aware that he was missing. Nobody had been told of an exercise where the students were playing *Where's Waldo?* with Dolby in the role of Waldo. They had instead spent the afternoon first playing team-building games and after that, working on a craft. The only person in the entire camp playing *Where's Dolby?* was Steele, whose hunch after the explosion was a correct one. He hid behind the dining hall door. When his whispers went unnoticed, he tried a different approach.

"Ouch," cried Adele. The wadded-up napkin that hit her in the face was more surprise than pain. She and Hope turned their heads to see Steele waving them into the hallway.

"What are you doing here?" Hope asked.

"I'm hiding out, keeping watch—I don't have a good feeling about this place right now. Have you seen Dolby?"

"Not since three o'clock."

"I was afraid of that. I think they may have kidnapped him," whispered Steele.

"No. Seriously? Why would they do that?" asked Hope.

"No idea," said Steele. "Look at this." After scanning the area first, he unzipped his pack to reveal a heavy, metal cylinder with a hole in each end. As they passed it back and forth, they asked what it was.

"It's heavy," observed Adele.

"I know. I texted a picture of it to my Dad's buddy who was in the Marines. He says it's a suppressor for an AR-15."

"Uh, speak English please?" Hope was talking for both of them.

"It's a silencer for an AR-15 rifle. You attach it to the end of the gun to make a semi-automatic weapon completely silent when fired."

"That can't be good," said a wide-eyed Adele.

"You think? I found dozens of them behind the Welcome Center. Also, check your phones. I've been texting you both the past hour."

"They took our cell phones. That's why we haven't been answering," said Adele. "I wonder if they are checking them. Steele—think hard. Did your texts give away that you are here at the Ranch?"

"I don't think so." He scrolled through his texts to check. "I think we're good. I just kept asking where you were and what you were doing."

Hope had an idea. "Hey! Keep that in mind. If something is being planned, and if they are checking our phones, Steele could feed them false information that might be helpful."

"Good idea," said Steele. "I'm going to keep looking for him. If I find anything out, I'll let you know."

5:33 p.m.

There were many other posters and banners and pictures covering the sick bay besides the one showing a boy's bare butt. Two of them caught Dolby's eye and gave him pause. The first looked like a hundred-year-old stitching that simply spelled out in cursive a verse from Psalm 46. "Be still, and know that I am God." The second was a photograph of an eight-point buck running through a stream next to the words from Psalm 42:1. It said, "As a deer pants for flowing streams, so pants my soul for you, O God." For the first time since their conversation about the barbershop quartets, Dolby wondered if God might be speaking to him.

29

TRAP

"The securest place is a prison cell, but there is no liberty."
—BEN FRANKLIN

6:27 p.m.

He tried to open the door again—still locked. He wasn't sure why he felt the need to keep trying. It had been three and a half hours of isolation. Dolby knew for sure now that this was no school exercise. He was being detained for some reason, but he sure couldn't figure out why. Another thing he couldn't figure out—how was he going to *search and rescue* anybody if he was locked up in a camp hospital? He tried to pry open the window, but it was permanently screwed in place. The screws, though, were not normal. Instead of a Phillips head or Flathead screwdriver, one would need a tool with a square-shaped end to unscrew them. Of course, there were none of those to be found. If he broke the glass, he would be heard. Besides, because of the way the building was situated, though he was on the second floor, it was technically the third level because of the walk-out basement. He would never survive a jump without breaking some bones. He planned to go to the police about his kidnapping if he ever got out of there. But then he remembered the beep. Uncle Veep had recorded him giving permission to hold him captive in this room for a game. They had his own words to use against him in case they were rightfully accused. But it really didn't matter at that moment. He was literally imprisoned with no way of escape. He could see now why this room was selected to be his jail cell. Speaking of bones, Dolby had another visitor and possibly some hope. He had to think fast, though. "Hey boss," mumbled Bones. "So, I guess that game them kids'er playin' is still running long. So, just sit tight for a mite." Dolby was surprised they thought he wasn't catching on. But he wasn't about to let Bones know that. "You need an'thang?" Bones often helped out with odd jobs at the Ranch on top of his night watchman duties.

"No, but I do have a couple of questions. Are you very handy?"

"Shoot, son. I can fix pert near an'thang. Sum'n broken?"

"Yeah, there are a few things that need an expert to fix. I was trying to get a band-aid earlier out of this drawer, but it's jammed." Dolby yanked on it a couple of times for affect. "Whoa—there it goes. Got it."

"What else ya got?"

"I think that window's busted. It's getting a little stuffy in here and I just wanted to open it a crack to get some fresh air." At the mention of the window, Bones grew visibly agitated.

"Oh 'bout that. Not sure I kin hep ya wit' it."

"Huh. I thought you said you were handy? I guess we found something you couldn't fix." Bones got agitated about that comment, too. Dolby was clearly pushing the right buttons.

"Oh, I can fix it—you best believe. I guess it won't hurt none to open it a touch." Bones played with the window until there was an inch or two of screen showing at the bottom. He grabbed a couple of nearby batteries and used them on each end to prop the window open ever so slightly. "See. I gotcha covered."

"Wow. Thanks mister. I can already feel a little breeze."

Bones seemed agitated once again. "Okay. Well, I best skeedaddle." Dolby's first instinct was to get the window open so he could yell out to somebody below. But the likelihood of that working was slimmer than Bones himself. His next idea, though, was genius. It wasn't without complications, but it was all he had at the moment. He untucked the whistle from his t-shirt—the perfect solution. The deer will hear the high-pitched signal and come to his rescue and the humans will hear nothing. Dolby inhaled deeply and muttered under his breath, "Here's hoping they believe it's a real emergency this time. I also hope they have worked through their differences."

It was free time until seven o'clock, so it wasn't out of the ordinary to see two girls and one boy talking in hushed tones under the pavilion. Other groups were under roof playing four-square, volleyball, and Knock-out. At one point, Hope realized something. She couldn't believe that anything could hold her attention while sports were being played nearby. But a plan was being hatched, and she was a part of it. There were a few things that had to fall into place for it to work. The most important of them required Steele to leave the Ranch. It was about a seven-mile bike ride back to downtown Gomer which would take about an hour to peddle. It was their best hope, so off he went. As he raced away on the road, other creatures, some four times his size, were racing through the woods in the opposite direction toward Gomer Ranch.

6:43 p.m.

With the whistle firmly in place between his front top and bottom teeth, Dolby turned his head to the side, and laid his cheek on the windowsill. After inhaling like he was about to plunge underwater for a long time, he exhaled and blew the whistle with all that he was worth. To be sure that it was heard, he continued to huff and puff as if trying to blow the house down. Feeling a little light-headed, he sank back, laid down on the cot, and waited. As he stared up at the ceiling listening for any noises outside, he suddenly remembered the last time he blew the whistle to call his deer friends for help. It ended up being an ambush meant to destroy them. What if he had just done that again? What if the reason he was locked up was to call the deer to the Ranch? What if they weren't after the journal at all, but wanted the whistle instead? Did he possibly just fall right into their trap again? If so, the deer would be the ones captured in their net. That same sick feeling at the pit of his stomach returned as he tried to keep pizza and pudding down. He was dripping with sweat and shaking. For the first time he hoped his deer friends would consider him to be the boy who cried wolf again and ignore his call. That hope was dashed seconds later when he began to hear activity below. He also felt activity below in his own stomach. For the first time all night, the puking boy was in the most appropriate room in camp.

At that moment, three cell phones in the possession of a raccoon half-tail all buzzed at the same time with a new text message from Steele.

30

REVELATION

"This book is a drama whose first character is the Infinite. Man is the second."
—VICTOR HUGO IN *LES MISERABLES* (1845)

6:49 p.m.

The outside commotion grew louder. Dolby forced himself to stand and take a look. He breathed a stinky sigh of relief that no deer were yet in sight. Instead, he gasped at the scene developing before him. From every direction, like rats scurrying in a sewer, came hundreds of raccoons. The high-pitched sound of the whistle must have also alerted the trash pandas to descend on what was now turning into a battlefield. The raccoons were using their nimble fingers and jaws to deposit random items in the area and then leaving to get more. Other masked bandits were piling the debris, trash, and branches into a barricade that was starting to extend the entire length of the back of the building. The animals were chirping to each other and scattering around as if their paws were on fire. Another voice—this one human—barked orders in a raccoon tongue from inside the basement. Just behind the blockade stood a picnic table. An adult with a gray hoodie and black ski mask to match the animals emerged to place what looked like a rifle on top of the wooden table. Dolby about fainted. A closer look revealed that it was a semi-automatic rifle. Whoever this was really wanted to destroy as many deer in as little time as possible. If the deer came by way of the cornfield to rescue him, they would be sitting ducks against such a powerful and high-speed weapon. If the animals rushed the gunman, the AR-15 was capable of shooting up to four rounds per second. Even in the outside chance that one of the bucks were able to get to him, there would be too many killed by then to make it a worthwhile plan. Besides, there weren't enough deer in Gomer to pull off something like that. Dolby also knew that it was too open in front of the building for an approach. They would certainly be coming through the cornstalks. The enemy knew that too. As if things couldn't get any worse, Dolby caught a glimpse of something that instantly made him as furious as his stomach had been minutes earlier. Alongside the swarming raccoons, dragging a barrier from the paintball field to add to the fortification, was none other than Speckles the deer. "You traitor!" Dolby yelled. The noise below had become so loud that there was no danger of being heard. "That's where you've been? Planning to attack your own kind alongside the enemy?!" If Dolby had the AR-15 in his perch at that moment, he was afraid of what he might do. Dolby glared at his former friend. "How could you?!" At that moment, almost as if he heard, Speckles sheepishly glanced up at Dolby's window. Upon making eye contact with the boy, the young buck with newly developing antlers immediately turned his head away and fled into the corn. This new development made Dolby feel even more helpless. Medical supplies were now flying across the room.

7:41 p.m.

Thankfully for Dolby, the deer had ignored his call thus far. The raccoons continued to fortify their fort, but at a much slower pace. For some reason, their enemy had not come as soon as expected. Meanwhile, a panting teenager arrived at a house in Gomer. Steele was out of breath both from the long ride, and also from his breakneck telling of the storm that was gathering seven miles away.

Sick of watching nothing happening, Dolby sank once again into the cot. Betrayed. It was a familiar feeling for him. He felt betrayed by his human friends who were nowhere to be found. He felt betrayed by his deer friends who had left him weeks ago. He felt betrayed by Speckles, who he thought to be a loyal friend. Sitting alone in a locked room helpless to do anything, he also felt betrayed by God. "Some search and rescue this has turned out to be." Hearing his voice echo made him feel even more alone. "If there's any rescue happening tonight, it won't be by me. I can't believe I am the one that needs to be rescued." At that thought, the boy sat up straight. He grabbed a pen and paper and began scribbling. He listed four thoughts down on the paper and stared at them. The first note read, "Rescue comes from above." His mind traveled back to the snake surrounded by a circle of fire. Its only salvation was from above; from someone else; from somewhere else. Salvation comes from above. The only way of real rescue is by God, he thought. The second written phrase took him back to the campground church service. "2 Chronicles 20," he said out loud. He was impressed that he had remembered. He pulled the old Bible off of the shelf, but it took him some time to find the verse. As he was flipping through the pages, it did not escape him that he had just voluntarily picked up the Bible for once because he actually wanted to. Once he found it, he read aloud.

> "O our God, wilt thou not judge them? For we have no might against this great company that cometh against us; neither know we what to do: but our eyes are upon thee. . .
> Thus saith the Lord unto you, Be not afraid nor dismayed by reason of this great multitude; for the battle is not yours, but God's."

The following thoughts flooded Dolby's mind: this battle is not mine. It never was. The battle belongs to God. I need to trust in *him*—not in myself, or my own abilities. Dolby then wrote down on the third line, "I will be watching you." Even though he felt alone and helpless, he knew in that moment that God was with him and watching over him. The last phrase written on the page were the two words sent as messages from Fantasma—"Search and Rescue." He wondered to himself if her messages had multiple meanings. Was he supposed to keep searching after the truth, but also at the same time supposed to search after God? "Maybe she intended that I seek the Windmaster first so that my deliverance would follow." These four truths made their way into Dolby's mind and heart in such a way that he felt waves of peace settle over him. He was still scared and nervous, but he was also now resting and trusting. He decided to read more. Opening the Bible to a random page, he read something so perfect for him at that moment; so comforting and timely, that the only conclusion he could make was that God indeed was there, was fighting this battle for him, and was watching out for his every need. Dolby had a new reason he wanted to be rescued—he just had to share that verse with Geema who alone with him would understand.

31

SURPRISE

"I got you to look after me, and you got me to look after you, and that's why."
—JOHN STEINBECK IN *OF MICE AND MEN* (1937)

8:27 p.m.

Below his window, the barricade grew higher, but the builders were growing restless. After he reached one hundred, he stopped counting the raccoons that were waiting both in front and behind the fortress. He had probably only counted half of them. If he could have seen as far as the horse barn driveway, he would have witnessed Steele and an adult get out of a vehicle. It was a relief to Steele to not have to make the bike ride back. The two met up with Hope and Adele at a conference room in the stable offices, which had become their battle planning headquarters. The rest of the seventh grade was gathered on a hill at the opposite end of camp for an astronomy learning session. Because of the darkness and being outside, Hope and Adele had no trouble slipping away. The kids were taking turns looking up at the stars through telescopes oblivious to what was happening down on the ground at the Welcome Center. Steele pressed *send* on his phone. Another text message appeared on the confiscated phones of Dolby, Adele, and Hope. All of the elements were almost in place to commence the rescue. It was now time to silently take their positions.

9:04 p.m.

If a deer rescue was unfolding, Dolby wished there was a way to call it off. He would not be able to live with himself if he were the cause of mass deaths of his friends. But he couldn't do anything. He was completely helpless to change the next hour or so. The boy kneeled down over the cot, bowed his head, and prayed earnestly with eyes open. He was still hopeful that all the time that had passed since whistling the alarm meant his call was being ignored. But a significant rustling below instantly shattered that hope. Hundreds of raccoons scurried around in order to man their battle stations. A human climbed to the top of the picnic table with rifle in hand. What was causing them to stir? Dolby could not see or hear anything coming from the cornfield. What he did hear was a non-stop barrage of strange-sounding instructions from the raccoon half-tail to his subjects. The masked man or woman raised a weapon and aimed it toward the cornfield. They must be hearing something. Dolby finally detected noises over the sounds of his quick breathing and pounding heart. An unseen army marched slowly through the cornfield toward the semi-automatic rifle. The closer the multitude got, the louder the sound of trampling cornstalks became. And the louder the sound became, the more Dolby and his enemy estimated the size of the arriving forces. When it seemed that the oncoming troops were on the verge of breaking through the corn and into open air, the marksman began firing his weapon as fast as his trigger finger could move. Back and forth he sprayed the cornfield with bullets. Corn cobs exploded. Corn stalks flew up into the air. To Dolby, it was like fireworks of green vegetation. No sounds were made by the gun, but the *pop-pop* sound of bullets hitting corn plants made it seem like the rifle actually had no silencer. The noise was now deafening, and Dolby could hardly watch. He expected the green fireworks to include the color red at any moment. But that moment never came. The rifle lowered. Bursting from the cornfield came hundreds and hundreds of creatures—only they were not deer. If the deer had mounted an attack without first sending shorter-to-the-ground animals, the whole herd would have been massacred. Instead, a blur of orange and black and white began attacking the gray and black of the raccoons. They were fox! Sly, sneaky, cunning little fox! The trampling sounds of corn plants was replaced by growls and barks and yips. Hundreds of fox and raccoon snapped their jaws and swatted one another all over the back lawn. Dolby immediately thought of his mom. She was coming to the rescue once again! The sniper raised his weapon but there was nothing he could do. Any shots fired now would also take out the precious trash pandas. Dolby could only stand by and watch. It began to seem like the fox were only there to create chaos and distraction and to keep the raccoons occupied. When they had opportunity to go for the kill, they backed off. The fox seemed to be toying with the night bandits. It was clearly the first phase of a bigger plan.

Steele and Karen Withers-Hart took their place on a hill overlooking the scene from the side of the building. She barked fox words of encouragement from the hill. Hope and Adele were hidden toward the back of the corn field awaiting their cue. They both sat on the backs of muscular animals who were chomping at the bit to enter the fray.

Dolby heard the unmistakable bugle call of Mortimer Moose acres away from the back of the cornfield. They came! Dolby's spirits immediately started to soar to think that foreign deer had arrived in Gomer for him. The Moose's trumpet cued a ground-shaking stampede. The galloping sounds now heard in the rows of corn made the fox army's approach seem like a few mice. The raccoon half-tail once felt invincible behind the thunderstick. Now, the thunder of the oncoming militia made his knees buckle. Even the earth seemed to shake with fear. Nonetheless, the human standing above the animal skirmish was determined to get his revenge. The gunman could have sprayed the cornfield with bullets like before, but he or she didn't expect to have to shoot so many times and was worried about having enough ammunition. Plus, he or she knew they had plenty of time—half of a football field— to take out all of the deer once they appeared in the open. Besides, the assassin wanted to see the looks on their faces when they died. A lone eye looked into the scope, the rifle was steadied, and a finger rested on the trigger. The animals burst out of the cover of the cornstalks, but no shots were fired. The sniper would not engage the weapon. He lowered it once again and couldn't believe his eyes.

32

STAMPEDE

"And he led them a great pace over rough and smooth and through thick and
thin, till the horses of all the courtiers were tired out and only these four were
still following. And they saw the stag enter into a thicket where their horses
could not follow. Then said King Peter ... 'Fair Consorts, let us now alight from
our horses and follow this beast into the thicket; for in all my days I never
hunted a nobler quarry.'"

—C.S. Lewis
in *The Lion, the Witch, and the Wardrobe* (1950)

9:22 p.m.

The sniper watched with bewilderment as wave after wave of 1,000 and
2,000-pound creatures emptied out of the corn and into the Welcome
Center backyard. Dolby, too, had not expected this. Deer he expected. But
not this. Stampeding into the cramped lawn were massive, muscular horses
from the horse barn. Of course, they would not be shot at either. That would
be too hard to explain. Behind the stampede sat Hope and Adele, each on
top of their own steed. Like cowgirls they corralled the horses into position.
The gunman dropped the weapon to his side and watched as dozens and
dozens of horses galloped around him and the raccoons and fox, who were
still fighting half-heartedly. The human on the table was so confused at the
development, that he didn't notice lines of other animals—this time the

expected deer—racing through the far sides of the cornfield in single-file. The first thing the largest of the bucks, moose, and elk did was to lower their antlers and, like construction bulldozers, completely demolish the fort that had taken the raccoon so long to build. Then, bucks and does of various colors and sizes began to form a circle around the horses and barricade. Dolby was as confused as the other half-tail. Total chaos kept him from opening fire on the deer. Approximately eighty-five horses were bumping into each other due to the small enclosure formed by the deer. Another deer entered the scene—the hated Speckles—this time to gesture to the nearest raccoon. Dolby watched the raccoon then jump up onto the table and relay a quick message to the assassin, who promptly gathered up his rifle and pushed his way through large bodies around the building and toward the front. Dolby suspected that more deer were arriving in front and Speckles was alerting his master. It was as the gunman was leaving that Dolby began to see the genius of the plan unfolding before him. Immediately, Shadow Muzzle and Gus made an opening in the circle for the horses to escape. Stallions, colts, mares, and fillies alike began to race around the building right behind the masked man. So many followed him that he could barely move. Once all of the horses, except for one, left the pen made by the deer, Shadow and Gus quickly reformed the gate so that just one horse was left inside. Dolby remembered back to that hot, sunny day baling hay at the Brown's. If one horse is left alone in an enclosed area, the rest of the horses will not run away. "They will stay close by!" Dolby thought that this would keep the killer boxed in long enough for someone to rescue him. At least that's what he hoped. By this time, the raccoon, weary from fighting, began to peel off and slink away into the darkness. "Cowards!" Dolby cheered. The fox also retreated toward Karen, licking their wounds. The deer who had formed a circle now turned to Dolby's window and began hopping, and bowing, and raising up their front legs, and making snorts and grunts that sounded a lot like cheering. The boy was soaking it all in when he jumped at a noise at the door. Rhythmic banging began in the hallway, reminding Dolby of a fireman with an ax tearing down a door. He would soon see that it wasn't a fireman. Instead, four small points of a young buck's rack, along with pounding hooves, began to tear through the wooden door. The more headway the deer made, the clearer it became—it was Speckles. Dolby grabbed a fire extinguisher—the heaviest thing he could find. He raised it above his head ready to slow an attack. The door splintered open. Dolby backed up. Looking bigger than Dolby had remembered, Speckles came at him. Dolby reared back the extinguisher.

"Half-tail! Half-tail! What are you doing? We don't have much time. Let's go!"

"Go where?"

"Anywhere but here. I'm rescuing you—hurry!"

"I saw what you did. You betrayed your kind."

"No. I was a spy for my kind! I infiltrated the enemy's camp so I could feed my deer brothers and sisters information about their plans. COME ON!"

Dolby hesitated. He still wasn't sure he could trust him, but the door *was* open. "Jump on!"

"Wait! Tell me who the mastermind is behind this attack."

"There's no time! I'll tell you everything later." Speckles was just fourteen months old. His muscles and bulk had not filled out yet, nor had his neck grown swollen with size like his elders. Despite looking kind of like a doe with nubs for antlers, he had matured to about 150 pounds and could transport Dolby short distances with ease. He held on to his neck for dear life as Speckles bounded down the flight of stairs and out the basement slider. The rest of the herd of deer were at that moment scattering back into the rows of corn, and Dolby saw why. A deranged, masked lunatic was running around the side of the building and firing off rounds. He had finally broken free from his horsey prison and was desperate for something to go his way. Thankfully, the horses were running wild now that the deer fence was no more. This gave Speckles enough time to sprint away from the bullets and toward the closest cover. At the edge of the cornfield, Speckles launched Dolby through the air toward the thick cornstalks. At that moment, a loud groan cried out through the night. A loud, painful groan. Somebody had been shot.

33

MISSION

"Old Dan must have known he was dying. Just before he drew his last breath, he opened his eyes and looked at me. Then with one last sigh, and a feeble thump of his tail, his friendly gray eyes closed forever."

—WILSON RAWLS IN *WHERE THE RED FERN GROWS* (1961)

9:47 p.m.

"NOOOOO!" squealed Snowflake. She ran toward the body, but Mortimer Moose beat her to it. Scooping up the listless body with his flat horns, he ran deep into the cornfield, away from the bullets. Wapiti carefully lifted the other unconscious body onto Shadow Muzzle's back, and they followed behind at a slower pace. Finding a clearing in a thickly wooded area, the bodies were gently placed in the dirt. Laying side-by-side were the Half-tail and the spy whose loyalty helped save him. Puddles of blood began to grow between them, but nobody could tell whose it was. Snowflake threw herself over both of them and sobbed. Now three creatures were covered in red. Dolby's mom arrived with a fox fleet behind her just in time to see Dolby stirring.

"Did we make it?" came the boy's mumble.

"Ssshhhh. Yes, dear. Just lay still and let me have a look." She was relieved to discover no injuries to her son. She wasn't as fortunate when checking out Speckles' condition. A bullet hole and oozing blood was evident in the young buck's torso. Snowflake sobbed even louder at the sight. Speckles opened his eyes slowly to see his Half-tail. "Half-tail! Half-tail! Half . . ."

"Sssshh. I'm right here."

"Am I departing to see the Windmaster?"

Dolby didn't think there was any reason to lie. "Yes, Speckles. Your work here is done. You saved my life and the lives of your friends. It is only time for rest now." Speckles tried to force a smile. Dolby was holding the deer's head with both hands. "Speckles . . ." Dolby said through tears. "Remember when you saved my life? That was awesome." With one last sigh of satisfaction, Speckles was gone.

Snowflake began licking the face of her friend. "I love you, Speckles." There were other casualties that night—a handful of raccoon and fox. No horses were lost, except in the sense that they were now frolicking freely around a couple of acres of camp. Multiple deer suffered gunshot wounds and injuries, but most survived. One whitetail from Ohio and two blacktail from Illinois lost their lives, but none hit harder than the passing of Speckles the spy.

After about twenty minutes, Dolby felt well enough to address the antler army. In a weary deer language, the boy thanked everyone for risking their lives to rescue him. He said that he never wanted it to be that way. He'd rather be the one doing the rescuing. But he realized something through the experience. "When one puts their own life on the line to save you, that is the ultimate expression of love. You have demonstrated love for me tonight that I can never repay. I promise that I will always be thankful; I will live in service to you all; I will never forget what you've done for me; I remain committed to all the deer species represented here." The deer erupted in grunts and snorts of approval. Just then, despite the darkness, two massive, light-gray figures emerged from the pines. He could only make out that they were caribou, but he could not tell who it was. A closer look revealed that it was Nanuk and Yukon, which could only mean one thing. Fantasma was near. Caribou were the guardians of choice of the great albino doe. But she normally had between six and eight caribou bodyguards. Maybe she wasn't near after all.

The male bull, Yukon, took over the meeting. "Friends. Greetings from Fantasma the Wise. We bring news from the north. In recognition of all you have done for this victory, you are to be saluted." The two lowered their massive horns. "We come also to recognize one of our number who gave his life for our sakes. He will never be forgotten. For all of history, according to Fantasma Bianca, this day will be known as *The Campaign of Speckles*." The deer responded by slapping the earth with their hooves, shaking their heads up and down, and snorting in unison. As deer mingled and basked in the victory, Dolby made a beeline to the caribou.

"Is Fantasma coming?"

"Maybe the great Fantasma already here," replied Nanuk.

"Is Fantasma really here?"

"Maybe our Fantasma not here but coming."

"So, you can't tell me?"

"The ways of the Albino cannot be tracked."

"I really need to speak to her."

"Actually, ready yourself. Fantasma has new message for Half-tail." Dolby hoped it would make more sense than the first two words. "She has one word for you—the message is *mission*."

"Mission?" Dolby asked, as if by asking it would make the message clearer. The caribou nodded. "Mission? *Search* and *rescue* and *mission*. Huh. Search and rescue mission? What?" Dolby racked his brain. "Could you now give her a message please? I really need to speak to her."

10:31 p.m.

Back at the Welcome Center, the masked murderer quickly and carefully cleaned up any evidence of the battleground. Dead bodies were tossed into the woods. Debris was piled up to be burned. AR-15's were put back under lock and key. He or she had gotten away with it. Their identity was never discovered and the secret of who had organized this was buried with Speckles. The girls snuck back into their cabins undetected during shower time and spent the next two days and nights reminiscing about mapping out the plan, riding the horses into battle, and saving Dolby and the deer. Despite the late hour, Steele rode his bike home. He was offered a ride home with the Hart's but welcomed some peace and quiet alone to reflect on the part he played. Having struggled for so long of not wanting to do the right thing, he was always surprised with how much more satisfying it was in the end to do what was right. Besides, he really didn't feel like going straight home anyway. There was a lot on his mind. Dolby, too, was not about to go back to the retreat. On the drive home, Mrs. Hart called Mr. Vanderflunder to inform him that Dolby had taken ill. Mr. V's comment that "Gomer Ranch has an excellent infirmary if he wants to go there first," was not a welcome suggestion.

34

HOME

> "It is always hard to see the purpose in wilderness wanderings
> until after they are over."
>
> —John Bunyan in *The Pilgrim's Progress* (1678)

10:45 p.m.

Even with the slam of the screen storm door, Geema remained asleep on the couch per her evening custom. She heard rumors that something was brewing at the Ranch. She had been aware of her daughter's departure with the pack of fox. Despite being worried sick about her grandson, daughter, and Snowflake, she still couldn't keep her eyes open. Dolby was excited to tell her the whole story, including the Bible verse he found for them. But he was equally happy for it to wait until morning. An exhaustion fell over him no doubt a result of the emotional roller coaster he had just ridden. He kissed his mom goodnight and creaked up the stairs to his room. The duffel bag plopped onto the floor. The sleeping bag flew across the room. The backpack bounced onto his bed. He was too tired to even place the items down gently. He, himself, fell back onto his bed. It was good to be home. It was also good not to be laying on a stiff cot. Out of habit, he reached for his backpack in order to look at his journal. Upon realizing what he was about to do, he pushed the backpack off of the bed. He no longer felt like thinking about suspects, their possible motives, and potential future danger. He had sought after that information for the past eight months and he was not much closer to cracking the case than he had been in February. He decided to give up. "If God wants me to find him or her, he's going to have to drop them into my lap. I'm done." He wondered what it would look like to seek after God first in his life. He suddenly wanted the journal for an altogether different reason. The boy rolled over onto his stomach in order to reach the bag on the floor. With head buried in his pillow out of fatigue, he felt for the zipper. He also felt around for the journal. He pulled it out and took one look and laughed. "Oops. I don't remember taking this!" The Bible from the infirmary bookshelf had made its way home with Dolby. He chuckled. "I wonder what God thinks about stealing a Bible?!" He reread Psalm 146:9 and felt a second wind to share it with his Geema. He also had second thoughts about grabbing the journal. He secured it, sat up in his bed, looked the suspect page over for the hundredth time, and promptly ripped the page out of the notebook. "It literally could be any of these people." In a fitting symbol of ending his search, the boy wadded up the paper into a ball and tossed it across the room.

11:54 p.m.

By now, Dolby was showered, completely unpacked, and finally ready to call it a day. After Operation Deer Preserve, or Half-Tail Triumph, the emotions were over-the-top. He was the hero. His planning was ingenious. He triumphed. He had saved the day. He was ecstatic with happiness. After the Campaign of Speckles, he wasn't the hero. It was the heroism of others that took center stage. So, the emotions were very different. He felt thankful, relieved, content, and full of joy. He was surprised that it didn't matter that he wasn't the knight in shining armor being paraded around for everyone to celebrate. The death of Speckles certainly contributed to his mood being somewhat muted. The knock on the door might as well have been antlers tearing through the entry for as much as it startled Dolby.

"Sheesh. You scared me! Come in."

"Sorry, dear. I thought you might want these after your long day." Geema entered gingerly balancing cookies on a tray and a glass of milk. "Your mom told me all about it. I was worried sick." She reached the plate out for him to take. Geema's chocolate chip cookies were the envy of Gomer.

"So worried that you fell asleep?" Dolby teased. She smiled and pulled the plate of cookies away.

"Just kidding! Thanks." He pried the plate away from her arthritic hands.

"Quite a treat of a retreat, huh?" she asked.

"I'll say. But usually when I think of the word *retreat*, I think of withdrawing and relaxing and getting away. It wasn't any of those things, although I guess I actually did get away in the end."

She sat down on the bed with a moan as old people do. "Is that yours?" She pointed to the Bible laying on the bed.

"Yep. Got it at camp. But that reminds me . . . you were right about something."

"I always am," she said with another smile and a pat on the leg.

"You sure were right about me not being able to do any of this on my own. I literally did nothing to help matters this time. I needed you to steer me in the right direction toward God. I needed Adele and Hope to plan for my rescue. I needed Steele to inform Mom. I needed my mom, all the fox, all the deer, and I especially needed God. You were right about seeking him first and not relying on myself. You were also right about his presence and guidance being everywhere like the barbershop quartet music. I think he actually was speaking to me during my short stay in the sick ward."

"That so?" Geema had perked up at the mention of how God had been working.

"When I was alone—well, first I realized I'm never alone. He is always there for me, and always watching over me. I opened up this Bible to a random page and God seemed to lead me right to a passage that felt at the time, and still does truthfully, that it was written specifically for me . . . and you!" Dolby grabbed the Bible. Geema noticed the bright pink sticky note sticking out. "It's Psalm 146:9. It says, 'The Lord watches over the sojourners; he upholds the widow and the fatherless, but the way of the wicked he brings to ruin.' Isn't that cool? It says that he takes care of the fatherless like me, and the widows, like you!"

Geema's eyes started to well up. "It's almost as if he offers himself as the perfect father for those who don't have dads, and as the perfect friend and husband to those who don't have one." She pulled him in for a big bear hug.

"You were wrong about one thing, though, Geema."

"Was I now?"

"Yes. You always say nothing good happens after midnight. Look at the clock." It blinked 12:03 a.m.

35

CELEBRATION

"Come along in, and have some lunch," he (the rat) said diplomatically, "and we'll talk it over. We needn't decide anything in a hurry. Of course, *I* really don't care. I only want to give pleasure to you fellows. 'Live for others!' That's my motto in life."
—KENNETH GRAHAME IN *THE WIND IN THE WILLOWS* (1908)

Dolby's mental energy had shifted. Instead of thinking day and night about questions like who the enemy was, what was the motive, what was the plan, and how could he stop them, he now was just curious about how all the parts came together for his rescue. "Remember," he had to remind everyone, "I was only an audience member to your show." Adele and Hope got back to the school from the Ranch in time to catch their regular buses home. Dolby couldn't wait any longer. He asked all of his friends—tailed and no-tailed—to join him for a celebration that evening at his treehouse. The two species were separated by about thirty feet with the humans up high in the tree fort and the deer down low on the ground. Nobody minded the separation for a couple of reasons. The first was that the two groups couldn't communicate anyway so it just made it less awkward. The second reason was the most important—the favorite foods of each were laid out for all to share. Inside the treehouse, Hope, Adele, and Steele enjoyed pizza, burgers, mac and cheese, salad, and Rice Krispy treats courtesy of Geema. The deer on the ground munched on pecans, hickory nuts, acorns, apples, blueberries, and blackberries. Dolby consulted with

Gus on the menu for his party. He insisted that poison ivy be included, maintaining that especially for the males, it was actually one of their very favorite things to eat. When Dolby broke the news that he was not going to go harvest poison ivy for obvious reasons, Gus would not back down. It wasn't until Dolby explained what would happen if the human guests got confused and started eating the wrong salad that Gus finally gave in.

His words of understanding? "They'd a been madder'n a cat gettin' baptized." Steele showed up late but made up for it by helping himself to three heaping plates of food.

"Thank you all for coming." The kids sat down on the 360-degree deck, while the deer rested below around the tree trunk. "I wanted to celebrate what each of you did to make the Campaign of Speckles such a great victory. By the way, the thought crossed my mind when I was locked up that you weren't coming at all, either because I had blown the whistle too much, or because of your being so divided."

"First of all," said Red Velvet, "our kind are much like the horse. We never leave one of our own behind. Secondly, it was your crisis that gave us the common goal to finally bring us back together."

"Makes sense. I also wanted a chance for all of you to say goodbye to our out-of-town guests." The teens clapped and the deer pawed the ground as the elk—Wapiti and Canuck, and the deer—Zayan and Saluja all stood as representatives of all the foreign deer in attendance.

Mortimer also stood representing the moose in attendance and bellowed, "moooooooooorrrrre!' when the applause started to die down.

"If you don't mind, could I take a few minutes to ask some questions?" He hadn't talked to either deer or school friends since he left the camp on Tuesday night.

A blacktail buck from the east coast answered for everyone in an entertaining fashion. "No suh, Bruh-thuh. Ya keep feedin' us this wicked good suppah and you kin ask questions 'til tomah-rah. This pahty here's a rippah."

Dolby started walking the circled deck as if he was speaking at a Circle of Nod. "My first question is . . ." he walked by Steele, which made him suddenly change his first question. "Steele—you were there! I saw you after it was over. How did you end up at Gomer Ranch?"

"I just had a hunch something was gonna go down during the retreat. So, I snuck over and just kept my eyes peeled. Once the explosion happened and I found a silencer for a rifle, I knew my hunch was right."

"So, you were responsible for alerting Mom and persuading her and the fox to come?"

"Yes," said Steele. The conversation between the two boys was not missed by the deer whose acute sense of hearing picked it up easily. Now, if only they understood English. "When we suspected your kidnapping, Adele, Hope, and I mapped out the rescue plan, but we needed the help of the fox. So, I left to recruit your mom and her fox friends. Believe it or not, they were already gathered and ready for the go-ahead. Apparently, word had gotten around from the deer of Gomer to the foxes—however that works. I outlined the plan of attack on the drive back to the camp and she quickly got all the fox on the same page. I also sent a couple of text messages in case the enemy was checking your phones. The first gave him the estimated arrival time of around 9 p.m. The second message sent just before that time said, "The deer will be arriving through the exact middle of the cornfield. Look for them to come right down the center."

Dolby laughed. "Good call! Or should I say, good text?!"

Realizing that he was leaving the listening deer out, Dolby addressed them with his next question.

"Then how did the deer find out about the kidnapping and the plot to lure you all to your deaths?"

Emboldened by the last speech from the East Coast deer, a doe from closer east—the Laurel Highlands near Pittsburgh, to be exact—spoke up.

"How's abaht yinze let me say't. I gawt this one. Jisabaht the time yinze was gathering dahn nair at the base camp, heres comes Speckles. And Jeez-o-man, he sez, 'Yainga bleevis.' And he goes in tells us abaht how he's been a-work'n as a spy, n'at. We 'tole him baht our plan t' storm through the corn cahbs, in he sez, 'don't go err. They gotz pahrful thundersticks a'waitin.' I sez to m'self, 'Well, scratch my back with a hacksaw. Mize well come up wit' a whole nutter plan.' That's when these here fahx shows up wit' the no-tail's battle idears. Yinze heard that and sez, 'get aht a tahn! Ahnno-dat's gone work. Airyago."

"Then how's comes . . ." Dolby laughed under his breath at how quickly he could adapt his accent to the one he was currently hearing. "I mean, how did Speckles come to be a spy in the first place?"

"Kimm-awn," came the reply. "No one really knows. Any yinze know?"

"Nobody knows for sure. Best guess," answered Wapiti, "is that Speckles wandered off, ran into the raccoons preparing for the campaign and just started helping without knowing any better. You know how much he loved to help. The enemy and the enemy raccoons probably took that to mean that he had switched allegiances and took his desire to help as intent to betray us. By the time he found out what they were planning to do, he was in too deep. But he came back again and again and told us everything. In turn, we told him to pretend he was on their side and to keep quiet, but to keep informing us of their plans. He was honestly happy to be helping both sides somehow."

"Did he ever tell anyone who was behind the attempted slaughter?" Dolby hoped somebody knew something. The entire herd was silent. "I was afraid of that. He was going to tell me but never got the chance." The whole assembly continued in silence until Dolby interrupted the silence again. "Oh, I've got another question." This time he was looking at his human friends. "Who is the horse half-tail?"

The kids laughed. "Nobody!"

"Huh? How is that possible? Somebody choreographed the movements of the horses. They surrounded the enemy; they stayed in his way; they kept him from firing on the deer."

Adele answered by saying, "I've raised horses my whole life. Let's just say I have a few tricks up my sleeve." Dolby made a mental note to revisit that question with Adele someday.

"One more question." Dolby stopped to think about how to phrase it. He couldn't figure out why the third message came *after* the mission was completed. "Does the world *mission* mean anything to anybody?"

36

MYSTERY

"Do you know when the mountain goats give birth?
Do you watch when the doe bears her fawn?"

—JOB 39:1

Much had changed in just three short weeks—the leaves, the weather, but had Dolby? Had Speckles and other fox given their lives in vain? He sure didn't feel any different, although he would have to admit that he thought a little more about God and a little less about himself these days. It was easy not to dwell on all of that with school and homework and activities in full swing. In fact, Dolby felt himself to be adventured-out and was content to take a break from any half-tail emergencies. He still didn't know what *mission* or *search and rescue and mission* meant, but he didn't much care right now. He was in recovery mode. With a belly full of lazy, Saturday pancakes and bacon, he laid on the living room floor googling Halloween costumes to the sound of clanging dishes. That's why he missed the first rap on the front door. After the second, Geema asked if he could get that. Dolby opened the front door to discover nobody there. He looked out to the right, middle, and left. Seeing nothing, he was reminded of the days when bullies would play *ding-dong-ditch'em* at his expense. But, when he closed the door, something unusual caught his eye on the welcome mat. A baby fawn sat on his front stoop all curled up on itself looking weak and helpless. Dolby left the baby in search of her mother who was hopefully nearby. He knew that mothers often left their babies alone so they could go feed and keep predators away. The scent of adult deer could attract predators to the baby, but babies could be left alone because they have no scent and cannot therefore be found by enemies very easily. As he looked around, he was thoroughly confused. First of all, it was the size of a newborn, but from the looks of her, she didn't show the normal signs of having just been born. Secondly, it was now October. Deer give birth in the spring and summer, with June being typically the latest. Was this deer sick and left here for them to take care of? He scooped up the little fawn and opened the door to go inside. When he turned, the deer squeaked as if she didn't want to go in that direction. Dolby shut the door and went around the house to the backyard. The nearest woods were off to his right, but when he headed that way, the baby let out another little shriek. "This is the weirdest game of hot and cold I've ever played," he said. The tiny creature led him straight ahead, over the fence, over the bridge of the creek, and straight into a thick group of pine trees. Still cradling the fawn, he pushed his way past prickly fir branches until the feeling of pine needles was replaced with a softer sensation. Now he saw white instead of green. Two giant caribou were now brushing up against him, acting as bodyguards in a walk forward. So tight was their proximity that Dolby was almost lifted off of his feet. They led him to another opening where six more caribou were stationed. The animals parted as he got closer revealing his mentor and guru, Fantasma the albino deer. He wanted to run to her but didn't know what to do with the load he was carrying. Sensing this, she made a motion with her head toward the ground, so Dolby gently placed the frail creature on a bed of flowers. Dolby yelled, "Fantasma!" and hugged the white and pink doe's neck. She looked at the fawn.

"Thank you, sweet Navi." With those words, the tiny deer stood up, caught a baby carrot tossed by Nanuk, and skipped away. "Navi is an oddity for our kind, just like me. She, however, is a dwarf and will never get as big or as tall as other whitetail."

"So, she was sent to bring me to you?"

"Correct, Half-tail." Dolby was still confused.

"Why couldn't you have just sent Snowflake to come get me?"

"Because I am the Phantom of the Wood, Fantasma Bianca the Wise, the Mysterious One, blown here by the winds of the Windmaster. How mysterious would it be to have someone just go fetch you?" They both laughed.

"I guess. I didn't even know you were here. And I would have thought you would have left by now. The Campaign of Speckles was over weeks ago."

"True enough, dear one. But there was more to be done. Like today's meeting."

"Thank you for the messages. I just wish I knew what they meant. Can you tell me now?"

"Not so fast," she snickered. "You humans are always in such a rush."

"First, I must hear your thoughts on the missives."

"The what?"

"The notes . . . the messages."

"Sorry—you are sometimes hard to understand. Well, at first, I thought that you were encouraging me to keep up the search for the enemy of the deer. I also thought you were calling me to prepare to rescue somebody or some animals. When that didn't happen—and I ended up being the one who needed to be rescued—I really didn't know what to think. And now that the word *mission* was added, I really am at a loss. Can I ask an awkward question?"

"Of course. You may ask anything."

"Why all the secrecy? Why couldn't you make your messages clearer so I could understand? I know that you are a mysterious being, but your messages didn't have to be, did they?"

"Young Half-tail. It was important in this crisis that you learn many lessons for yourself. If your mother or grandmother or I just told you the lesson you are supposed to learn, it would not last; it would not land permanently in your heart. You needed to arrive at the truth yourself for it to endure. Also, it is clear that you rely on yourself too much, and you needed to see your need of the help of others. By the way, that is the way of the Windmaster, is it not?"

"What do you mean?"

"Do you always know what he is doing? Does he always make himself clear? Does he not withhold things from you so that you will pursue him? Does he not ask you to trust him even when you do not understand?"

There was quiet in response to that. Dolby was thinking about past conversations with Geema; about old Sunday School lessons; about previous journal entries, and then had a thought to add to the argument.

"And Jesus—er, the Windmaster's Son—even spoke in parables. Stories that often revealed truth to some about the Windmaster's kingdom, but also hid the truth from other listeners all at the same time."

"Exactly. You are to seek him for all of your answers. If you are just spoon-fed the answers, you will have no need for him or anybody else."

By this time, Dolby knew where this was headed. "You're not going to tell me what *mission* means, are you?"

For the first time in the conversation, the albino deer smiled and kept her mouth shut.

37

RACE

"The brave things the wonderful folk of the stories went out and looked for,
because they wanted them, because they were exciting and life was a bit dull,
a kind of sport, as you might say. But that's not the way of it with the tales that
really mattered . . . Folk seem to have been just landed in them, usually—
their paths were laid that way."

—J.R.R. Tolkien in *The Lord of the Rings:
The Two Towers* (1954)

The weekend before Halloween was traditionally Fall Festival at the
Gomer County Fairgrounds. Dolby, Steele, and Adele had great child-
hood memories of hayrides, haunted houses, corn mazes, pumpkin carving,
costume contests, and the petting zoo every fall. Dolby and his mom made
it a point to always visit Geema during Fall Festival. Hope, of course, always
had a tournament. This year, however, was going to be different, according
to Swampy Canis, Clayton and Carol Brown, and Karen Withers-Hart. For
years and years, the adults went to the festival for their children—to only do
kid stuff. Now that the kids were older, it was the parents turn to choose the
activities, whether the teens liked it or not. One of the major draws was the
annual open drag racing competition, and this year, the parents dragged the
kids to watch. Of course, they had to bribe them with a trip to the conces-
sion stand like they were five years old. And of course, it worked. Practice
rounds were just finishing up on the asphalt track when the group took

their seats under the grandstand. The teenagers found it more entertaining than they expected since the event allowed people to bring any vehicle they wanted to race, provided at least one other person signed up to race that same machine. There were contests between four-wheelers, motorcycles, cars, trucks, and their favorite—John Deere tractors.

"Too bad Peev didn't bring his golf cart," remarked Steele. The event started at seven and became increasingly competitive as the night wore on. Organizers saved the best races until later in the evening to ensure the most spectators for those events. For the kids' money, though, it was going to be hard to beat two old coots charging down the home stretch neck-and-neck on riding lawn mowers. It seemed to Dolby that the whole town was there—he had seen Bones, Uncle Veep, Peev, Enid, Mildred, Mr. V, Jed, Officer Robinson, Chief Kowalski—it was a veritable who's who of the Gomer VIPs. Geema stayed home because she didn't want to miss her stories. Of course, he was overestimating. If the whole town of Gomer, Michigan were there, the stands would have been filled with almost 1,600 people. To be more accurate, there may have been one-fourth of the town in attendance. But also, to be fair to Dolby, when the last race of the evening was announced, the swell of cheering sounded like the applause of 1,600 people. Since the teens and their parents weren't regular attenders of the Gomer Drag Races, they had no idea why these last two participants were getting such an ovation. Dolby looked around and noticed not a single person still sitting down. They could not make out the identities of the drivers since they were outfitted from head to toe in race driving gear, and the racing helmet kept them from seeing their faces. Neither car looked familiar, or did they? Steele thought that maybe he had seen the red one before, but couldn't be sure. He looked around to ask his dad but Swampy was nowhere to be found. The cars were now fifty feet behind the starting line. The muscle cars revved their engines. Both spun their tires until smoke poured out behind them. The kids had learned earlier in the night that drivers do burnouts like that before the race in order to heat up the tires and make them softer and stickier to give them more grip on the racetrack. A white Dodge Charger inched up to the starting line and stopped perfectly even with the red Chevelle.

The loudspeaker reverberated with instructions for the drivers. "Wait for all three lights to go yellow at the same time." The crowd erupted in anticipation. When one light, two lights, then three lights went off, so did the souped-up stock cars. Side-by-side they screamed down the quarter mile drag strip. The entire race only lasted twelve seconds, but the crowd didn't mind. The red Chevrolet pulled away at the very end to win both the victory and the hearts of the cheering race fans. The stands emptied to join some kind of a celebration down at the finish line. The Brown's, Hart's, and Steele did not understand. They began to ask questions.

"Why is this such a big deal?"

"Who is that anyway?"

"Why weren't the other races this important?"

"There's got to be a story, right?"

A gray-haired gentleman with a veteran's hat and baggy clothes was among the last to leave due to his advanced age. He overheard the questions and decided to get involved.

"Hello. Couldn't help but hear some of your discussion just now. Haven't you been reading the Guardian?" Everyone shook their head no. "That there's the best drag racer ever come outta Gomer in fifty years easy. Shoot, back when he was only in high school, he was winning regional races, the state competition, and went on to race nationally."

"Well, I'd say he's still got it," remarked Mrs. Brown.

"Seems that way."

"But why all the extra enthusiasm?" asked Karen.

"Well, see, there was this terrible accident, and it really got to him. It was so traumatic that he could never bring himself to race again until tonight. And you were all witnesses!" He clapped his hands with delight.

"That must have been some drag racing accident, huh, sir?" asked Mr. Brown.

"Oh. That's the thing. It didn't actually happen on an official drag racing course. His car was fine, and he didn't even suffer a scratch. It was just a bad scene and he was never the same. Must've been late '70s. He hasn't raced in forty or more years! So, this here really is something of a feel-good redemption story."

Dolby began to connect some dots. "Sir, did somebody . . ."

He was interrupted by the roar of the crowd and the old man yelling, "There he is!"

Dolby, Steele, and Hope couldn't believe what they were seeing. The man peeled his racing helmet off to reveal a shiny, sweaty, bald head. Smiling from ear to ear and high-fiving fans was none other than Peev Vanderflunder!

"Wow—not who I was expecting," commented an impressed Steele. He looked around to share the moment with his absent dad.

"That's Barney's boy, Percy. Well, good for him. Have a good night, folks." The old man turned to go. Dolby stopped him.

"Excuse me sir . . . um . . .thank you for your service. Also, may I ask one more question."

"Certainly, son."

"That accident—did somebody, say a friend of Percy's, happen to die that night so long ago."

"So, you *have* heard of it. It was a terrible tragedy. Forever altered the courses of the lives of a lot of folks." The old man looked down, shaking his head. "Such a shame. Okay folks, drive safe."

Dolby's friends were not tracking with his train of thought.

"Guys, we've got some research to do. Something may have just gotten dropped into our laps."

38

DIRT

"...but it's wrong what they say about the past, I've learned,
about how you can bury it. Because the past claws its way out."

—KHALED HOSSEINI IN *THE KITE RUNNER* (2003)

Even though it was late when they got back, the teenagers convinced their parents to let them stay out even later. They had to recheck the old evidence from Operation Deer Preserve. Back in the vault underneath the underground railroad for abused dogs, they searched through the clues. The hand-drawn calendar of January and February was still visible on the whiteboard. Also still readable was a red circle around the date *February 14* with a connecting line to the phrase, *40th anniversary of Joe's death*. Joseph Krantz had been killed in a car accident when a buck jumped out in front of his car. This was the event that caused Edith and Cliff Krantz to break both from reality and the law in a failed crazed revenge attempt to destroy Gomer deer for taking their son. The item Dolby was looking for was once taped to the bottom of the whiteboard. "Where did it go?"

The teens scrambled around the coal cellar to find it. Steele was looking hard, but not for clues. Instead, he kept looking at the stairs and up at the door that connected the main level to the basement. "Wait," Adele finally asked, "what exactly are we looking for?"

"The old printout from the Guardian newspaper."

"This?" asked Hope, holding up a small piece of paper, smudged from the dirt floor.

"That's it!" Dolby grabbed the article and began to refresh himself about the accident. The kids looked over his shoulder as they all reread the obituary from 1978.

> GOMER, Joseph Krantz, 16, of Gomer Township passed away last night at Gomer General Hospital from head injuries resulting from an automobile accident on Booger Hollow Road at approximately 10 p.m. on Friday, February 14. Krantz was driving home from a Gomer High School basketball game, where he starred on the court for the past two years. Even though alcohol is not thought to be a factor, it is believed that Krantz was driving too fast for the stretch of road that is often used as a drag racing track for local boys. Nobody else was in the vehicle and no word on whether another driver was involved. However, the blue Buick Skylark was found in the ditch completely totaled with a dead and bloodied eight-point buck discovered nearby, leading local authorities to believe that the ultimate cause of death was a whitetail deer leaping in front of the car. Police are continuing the investigation. Krantz is survived by his mother, Edith, and father, Cliff, both of Gomer. Visitation and funeral arrangements are forthcoming.

"I don't get it. What does this have to do with Peevy?" inquired Adele.

"This may be a shot in the dark but read between the lines here—it makes sense. It occurred on Booger Hollow Road where everyone drag-races. There was no collision with another car, but the investigation leaves open the possibility that another driver was nonetheless present. Isn't it possible that Peev and Joe were drag racing that night when the buck jumped in front of Joe's car? If Peev witnessed the death of his friend because of a deer, that could have traumatized him enough to quit racing. I wouldn't want to race again if my drag racing was partly responsible for a friend's death."

"Yeah, and the old guy at the track said that he hadn't raced in over forty years. That puts the date in the late 1970s," said Hope.

"Steele, do you remember what year his Chevelle is? Could that be the car he used back in '78?"

"Wait. What?" Steele was attempting to see out through the basement glass block window and was clearly distracted by something else.

"Peev's car—what year is it? Did he ever say?"

"It's a 1970."

"Do you think it could be the car he used back in 1978?"

"Oh, yeah. I'll bet it is. Remember when I asked if we could ride it to Uncle Veep's the night he showed us his stuffed deer collection? His exact words were, 'It's not something I drive around anymore.'" Steele continued the logic. "So, maybe Peev was working with the Krantz's the first time around. When the plan failed and they were put away in jail, it was up to him alone to avenge his friend's death."

"Which would explain all the Vanderflunder visits to her. They were plotting a different way to get revenge on the deer," added Adele. "Think back also to when Peev showed us the secret lair. He was trying to get us to think his brother was the enemy and not him."

"Plus, he seemed to have a perverted joy in showing Red, Gus, Shadow, Monster, and Snowflake the heads of their friends mounted on a wall." They all nodded at Dolby's observation. "He wanted to make sure they came with us, twisted jerk."

"Also, remember the whole incident caused the deer in Gomer to begin fighting. Could part of the plan have been to weaken them by causing division in their ranks?" They all nodded at Adele this time. "But can we say that Peevy is our raccoon half-tail? Does he share characteristics with them?

"I think we can say for sure that he is sneaky and creepy," said Steele.

"And unpredictable and dirty," added Adele.

"Yeah—and possibly destructive," Hope interjected.

"Do we have enough evidence to bring in Officer Robinson, though?" wondered Dolby.

"We could always sit down with him and see what he thinks?" answered Adele.

Dolby thought again of past interactions with Peev and shuddered. Maybe he had been watching him all this time after all.

Steele also seemed nervous. "Yeah. Let's get outta here."

39

WARRANT

"It is quite possible that an animal has spoken to me and
that I didn't catch the remark because I wasn't paying attention."

—E.B. White in *Charlotte's Web* (1952)

O fficer Kyle Robinson talked into the receiver at a desk piled high with papers and files. Four teens waited patiently in chairs. "I'm sorry ma'am but there's no law against it. No. Playing basketball in one's driveway cannot be considered disturbing the peace." The policeman rolled his eyes at the kids and sighed. They could hear a high-pitched voice on the other end going a mile a minute. "Well, okay. If it happens that late next time, you can give us a call. *But only after talking to the parents first.*" He hung up the phone and explained after another eye roll. "It's that exchange student from Latvia playing basketball too much and too loud again." The small-town cop was up to his eyeballs in work. "You wouldn't think in a place the size of Gomer we'd ever be this busy. Look at all this." He picked up one file— "kids shaving Coach Blitzer's dog and painting it like a skunk." He shuffled through the pile and showed them another file. "Spray painting the overpass. And look here—silo tipping. At least you teenagers are providing me with job security." So busy with work, Officer Robinson barely listened to the four kids sitting right in front of him. They were separately thinking that after leading him to the arrest of the Krantz's that they'd earned more of his attention. Dolby gave him the story anyway. "Ummm hmmmm," hummed the officer staring at his computer screen and pecking away at the keyboard. Dolby, Steele, Adele, and Hope had walked into the Gomer Police Station earlier as if they owned the place. They strutted right past the officer on duty at the front desk, who looked up from her paper, and simply shrugged. "Are you sure? Is that so? Interesting." He wasn't interested. It wasn't until Steele pulled something out of his backpack that Robinson made a double take and stopped working. "Where did you get that?" He reached for the item.

"That's what we're trying to tell you," emphasized the once shy Adele.

The kids now had his interest. He ran his fingers along the metal tube and squinted to read the tiny lettering on the side. "This is a homemade suppressor for an AR-15. Did you know that? The parts can be bought illegally over the internet. Where did you find this?"

They proceeded to tell him the whole story of Peev's ambush, his using a semi-automatic weapon on camp property, about killing Speckles. "So, it's not illegal to purchase and use an AR-15 in Michigan yet. It's also not illegal to use silencers like this. But, whenever someone builds their own, it's a major red flag. These babies are among the most highly regulated gun accessories out there. You've got to apply for a license, pay a huge fee, and submit to extensive screening. It can take more than a year to go through the whole process. So, the people who buy these off of the black market are trying to hide something—they either don't want a record of the purchase or don't want to submit to a criminal background check. Stuff like that. Tell me more." After they were finished, he thought for a minute. "With your testimonies, and the presence of illegal silencers, that may be enough to get a search warrant. I'd like to see if we can track down those firearms to see if they are legally registered."

It was a statement designed to signal the kids that the conversation, though important, was now finished. Instead of being one less thing on his plate, the meeting with the kids just added more for Officer Robinson to do. However, they didn't pick up on the signal. In their minds, there was one more very important matter to discuss. "Absolutely not," was the feedback they received from their proposal. "That would not only be highly abnormal, it would also be borderline inappropriate." But the kids would not be deterred. Steele spoke for the four of them. "Just keep an open mind about it just in case."

To that, the officer would only say, "I can't imagine any scenario where I could okay such a thing. Nothing would be more unprofessional." But, in order to get them off of his back, his last words to them were, "Tell you what. I will not close the door on that, but, if I can be completely honest, it is so unlikely that the door is probably mere inches from being closed." That little bit of hope was enough for the junior detectives.

For the next week, Officer Robinson jumped through hoops to obtain a warrant from the judge with the hope of finding enough evidence to arrest Peev. He had to provide written affidavits and probable cause paperwork to convince the judge that there is reasonable suspicion to search Gomer Ranch. Meanwhile, Steele was jumping through his own hoops on another project. He met separately with Uncle Veep, the Brown's, Chief Kowalski, and even the mayor to see if there was enough need and interest to proceed.

During the week of waiting, Dolby caught up on journal entries. He added new quotes that he had read in books, magazines, and the internet to the quote journal. One night, as he sat in bed entering them, he stopped, thought about something for a few minutes, then grabbed the blank notebook still left in his backpack. He scribbled down something on the first blank page. He transferred some quotes from the old book into the new. He opened his Bible. He made internet searches on his phone. From then on, whenever he wrote in his new journal, he never did so without having the Bible and his phone nearby.

40

ARREST

"There were two sets of encyclopedias that had sections on rats. From them
we learned that we were about the most hated animals on earth, except maybe
snakes and germs. That seemed strange to us, and unjust . . . But people think we
spread diseases, and I suppose possibly we do, though never intentionally, and
surely we never spread as many diseases as people themselves do."

—ROBERT C. O'BRIEN
IN *MRS. FRISBY AND THE RATS OF NIMH* (1971)

With search warrant in hand, Officer Robinson, along with his new
partner Officer McGregor, drove the squad car down the long, tree-
lined driveway to the front of Gomer Ranch. It was eight in the morning
and they wanted to start their day delivering the summons. Bones was the
first to greet them having just finished a shift at the Hideaway. He didn't
know the whereabouts of Percy Vanderflunder. Steele's description of the
gun locker behind the basement at the back of the Welcome Center was
spot on. The two officers found it locked with a padlock. When Bones
couldn't produce the key, McGregor used a bolt cutter to break the latch.
They opened it slowly to reveal a cache of different types and sizes of weap-
ons. "I don't think these are for paintball," commented Robinson. They
confiscated each gun carefully in order to avoid disturbing any fingerprints.
As the guns were transported to the front of the building, four kids arrived
via bicycle. Officer McGregor was new to Gomer and the force so when

he approached the kids to shoo them away, Kyle Robinson stopped him. "Believe it or not, they are the reason why we have a truck full of AR-10s and 15s right now. Guys—you can stick around, just stay away from the investigation." They nodded. "McGregor, why don't you run the serial numbers on those rifles, and I'll keep searching. Maybe one of us will find something so we can arrest this weasel right on the spot." Officer Robinson took notes and pictures of hundreds of bullet holes in the backyard trees and picnic tables—evidence that rounds had been fired illegally in a protected area. Robinson said aloud to nobody in particular, "Why would anybody be firing shots, let alone this many, at a camp and conference center?" After forty-five minutes, McGregor approached Robinson and handed him a report on a clipboard. The detective flipped through three pages. "Interesting. I think we've got plenty to proceed."

"I think we've got some viable fingerprints on the rifles as well."

"Okay. Let's go get 'im." The watching teenagers rightly assumed the rifles weren't legally registered. Just like the silencers, Peev would have needed to clear a background check and have records of purchase from a federally licensed dealer. Ironically, Peev was now hidden away in the camp infirmary hoping to avoid detection, and to watch the events unfold below. He seemed like nocturnal vermin more than ever. Nothing, it seemed, would spook him from his place of hibernation. Nothing, that is, until four kids who ruined his second revenge attempt turned the corner and came into view. At the sight of them, Peev lost control. He pried open the window as Bones had done before and began to yell uncontrollably at the Half-tail and his friends.

"How dare you interfere with me! Don't you know I am a Half-tail? You screwed up forty years of planning—TWICE!" His rantings became louder and crazier the more they stood there looking up with stunned faces. He ranted long enough for the policemen to take action. They found the room with the repaired door easily and promptly handcuffed him and began to read him his rights.

"You have the right to remain silent . . ."

"You are arresting *me*? Do you know what those kids and those deer did to my life?"

". . . anything you say can and will be used against you . . ."

"My friend is dead. That means nothing to you?"

". . . in a court of law . . . "

"Raccoons are dead. They did it. Why aren't you arresting them?"

"You have the right to an attorney . . ." The bald man was now fully out-of-control, acting like a cornered, wounded, rabid raccoon himself. Robinson was now outside guiding him toward the squad car with Dolby, Steele, Adele, and Hope looking on.

"I am a raccoon Half-tail," he insisted. Of course, this made him seem even more loony to the policemen.

Steele couldn't help himself. It was a mistake to think that he could stand by silently. "You mean you're a half-tail to trash pandas."

Peev exploded. "Trash pandas? TRASH PANDAS? They are not trash pandas! They like to be called treasure cats! I should have shot you when I shot those deer!"

Officer Robinson calmly checked his body camera to make sure it was recording. "Looks like he wasn't interested in taking advantage of his Miranda Rights."

"Looks like his words *will* be used against him in a court of law, too," whispered Dolby loud enough for Peev to hear.

"Why you . . ." Peev's arms flailed behind him as he attempted to wriggle free from the grip of the policeman. "How dare you! Do you know who I am? I am a true Half-tail. I am a championship drag racer. Where is your respect?"

Steele was the first to ask. "Please, Mr. Kyle?" Kyle Robinson knew exactly what Steele was asking—it was in reference to the last conversation they had back at the precinct.

"You know I can't do that. We've talked about this."

"You always were a coward," Peev said to Officer Robinson. "I knew when you were growing up you wouldn't amount to anything. How's the missus?" Peev prodded the cop further. "She left you yet? Everyone knows you're having problems." At this point, the convict was desperately trying to push his buttons.

"Aw, come on. Why not?" Steele begged. The cop ignored his pleas. He was too busy struggling to secure the criminal. Steele asked again. "Pleeeeease?"

"I could get into some serious trouble. You know that. I have to remain professional, Steele," the policeman said with voice raised and through clenched teeth trying to get him into the backseat.

"Hah!" yelled Peev. "Professional like your dad always was?" Robinson's father owned a general store in town but was accused years ago of arson when it burned to the ground. Nobody could ever prove anything, but the rumors were that he had burned it down himself to collect the insurance money. It was a painful family memory made even more painful by the fact that it was not true, but widely believed.

"Okay. That's it. I've heard enough. I tried. You watched me try. I am not responsible for what happens next." He gave a knowing look toward the four teenagers. The officer finished wrestling Peev into the back seat of the squad car and closed the car door, but not completely. He left it open a crack and looked around. After giving the kids a nod, Officer Robinson turned his back to the car and raised his hands up in the air still steaming while everyone watched and waited. "You brought this on yourself, buddy," he muttered under his breath. "This is on you, not me." Sure enough, not thirty seconds later, a black and white creature waddled out of the cover toward Peevy. The policeman opened the car door another crack and faced away once more. The skunk turned methodically and faced away from the raving lunatic who was now crying, "No! No!" Stinkerbelle would not be discouraged. She flipped up her tail and accurately hit her mark with a sulfur-smelling pepper spray. Even the two officers couldn't keep from laughing.

41

SEEDS

"You cannot have Jesus' rescue without accepting his rule."

—TIM KELLER

A few days later, Dolby came home from school, stepped onto his front porch, and knew instantly what Geema was making. The unmistakable aroma of freshly baked pie drew him inside as if a bloodhound hot on a trail. "What kind? What kind?" When Geema baked pie, it was such a big job that she always ended up making more than one.

"I've only made one so far. Can't you guess?"

"I'd say blueberry?"

"Close. Raspberry rhubarb." She was rolling the dough for the second crust. "This one here will be pumpkin."

Dolby's shoulders slumped. "Awesome." He hated pumpkin pie. He considered it the fruitcake of Thanksgiving. "Why are you making pumpkin so early?"

"I figured we have all these Halloween pumpkins for decoration, we might as well make something useful out of one of them before they go bad. In fact, how about if you make yourself useful, dear, and scoop out the seeds for me." She pointed to the orange squash. "While you do, tell me about Dolby Brad." He was already slicing a circle at the top of the gourd with a wide chef knife.

"Mainly just relieved. I didn't think we'd ever figure out who was behind all the no good. It's so nice that he is in custody and not out there planning another attack."

"You feel safer now?" Geema asked with flour caked throughout her face wrinkles.

"Yep. I really do. I guess I didn't know how much stress the whole thing was causing. I'm able to have fun again and I'm sleeping better."

"The Lord gives sleep to those he loves," she said.

"Huh?"

"The Lord gives sleep to those he loves. Psalm 127:2."

Dolby laughed. "You should've been a preacher. You can turn anything into a sermon."

She considered his comment. "I guess it's just that barbershop quartet principle again—He is everywhere; His truth is everywhere. He's working all the time. He speaks all the time. We just have to have the ears to hear it." She caught herself starting to preach again. "And I don't turn everything into a sermon." She blew flour at him.

"Yes, you do. I'll prove it," challenged Dolby. "He scooped out stringy, slimy guts from inside the pumpkin. "Okay. Look at all of this in my hands. Apply the first spiritual thing you can think of."

"That's easy," she said barely looking up. "We are like pumpkin guts in God's hands. Despite our sin and ugliness, He cleans us up and keeps us in the palms of his hands. Like Jesus said, 'I give them eternal life, and they will never perish, and no one will snatch them out of my hand.'" She laughed. Dolby separated the seeds from the muck and showed his grandmother the pile of pumpkin seeds.

"Alright. Do this."

"Hmmm. That's a little tougher . . . but, I think I've got it."

"Of course, you do."

"This is a little out there, but it works. You know how you and your friends are always seeing who can spit watermelon seeds and pumpkin seeds the farthest? Well, the book of Revelation says that he knows when we are neither cold nor hot for him. Then he says, 'Because you are lukewarm, and neither hot nor cold, I will spit you out of my mouth.'"

"It really says that?" Dolby was surprised.

"Yep. And look, I'm no preacher, but I think he says that not because we are ever in danger of getting pushed away. The rest of the Bible makes it clear that, like I said, no one can snatch us out of his hands. No, I think it has to do with commitment. When he saves us, he wants our whole heart. He wants our all; our complete trust. He doesn't want us riding the fence." She could hear herself sermonizing again but it was too late—the train had left the station. "You been riding the fence, Dolby?" They both knew the answer, but Dolby changed the subject once again, or so he thought.

"Maybe. Hey! Since we are talking about spiritual things, what do you make of the messages I was sent during this whole thing?"

"Remind me again?"

"*Search. Rescue. Mission.*" It had been such a mystery for so long, Dolby actually thought something was going to finally stump Geema.

"Oh, that's easy," she said matter-of-factly. "Sure. You know how this time you were the one being rescued and not doin' the rescuin'? Well, never forget how that felt. You were humbled, were you not? You were thankful and wanted to show your thankfulness to those that saved you, yes?" He nodded. "Is it safe to say you have a new, stronger commitment to your friends for what they did for you?" He nodded again. "Okay, here me out. *Search*—God wanted you to learn to seek him first and so he put you in a position where all you had was him. *Search and rescue*—your rescue came only after you sought him and prayed. You learned you were the one needing to be rescued and not the one who was to do the rescuing. When Jesus rescues someone from their sins, he calls them to commit their whole lives to him in thankfulness and service and worship for what he's done for them. That's where the *mission* comes in. This was not about your mission to catch Peev. Did you notice the *mission* message came *after* you had been rescued? That tells me that God has a mission for you to serve him with your whole life out of love for what he's done for you. When God sent his son to die for you, it was his *search and rescue mission* to save you. Now you are tasked to continue that search and rescue mission in your own life, and in the lives of others. He is asking you to be hot for him and not lukewarm." She paused, and smiled, and asked him to pass the spatula. Even she had impressed herself this time. "Did you hear what I just said? It's important to me that I know you heard what I just said."

"I was listening, Geema. What part? You said a lot."

"About continuing that search and rescue mission in the lives of others."

"Yeah, that. I heard that."

Geema was trying to be diplomatic. "Well, honey. I'm afraid you've missed a lot of clues when it comes to one of your friends."

"I have? How so? I guess you're right, because I really have no idea of any problems my friends are going through right now."

"Well, I am not at liberty to share any of it with you. You've got to uncover the clues yourself. But I will help you get started. As you try and unveil the signs, I suggest you don't invite Steele to help you."

42

SWAMPY

"You don't really suppose, do you, that all of your adventures and escapes were
managed by mere luck, just for your sole benefit? You are a fine person,
Mr. Baggins, and I am very fond of you; but you are only quite a little fellow in
the wide world after all!"

—J.R.R. Tolkien in *The Lord of the Rings:
The Fellowship of the Ring* (1954)

Adele and Dolby laid on a dusty barn floor and stared up at cobwebby
rafters. Dolby tossed a tennis ball up and down in silence. Zeke's eyes
tracked the ball's movement as if he were a police dog watching a criminal.
They had laid there throughout the sunset and very little had been said. The
only time sound echoed through the second floor of the barn was when
Dolby tossed the ball into the bales of hay piled at the far end. Zeke would
tear away in search of the treasure among the rectangles of hay and bring
it back for more.

"Are you sure she said it was Steele that was having problems?" This
was the third time Adele asked the same question, each time in a different
way.

"She didn't come out and say it exactly like that. But she did advise me
not to include Steele in this conversation. So, what else could she mean?"

"Right." Adele was as stumped as Dolby. "But Steele hasn't acted any
different lately, has he?"

"I don't think so. I mean, we would notice something like that."

Adele chimed in again. "So, what exactly was the context of the conversation?"

"Geema was trying to get me to see that I need to pay attention to others because part of my purpose as a Christian is to continue God's search and rescue mission in the lives of others. Then she used Steele as an example of somebody that I have ignored and missed clues about." More silence followed.

If they hadn't been used to the eerie creek of each wooden step, they would have been frightened at the noise of someone approaching. The light outside was fading fast, so they could not tell at first whose silhouette now joined them. It only took a couple of smooth strides to recognize the athletic gait of Hope. "Your mom said you guys were up here!" Her enthusiastic greeting was an odd contrast to their somber mood. "What's going on?" She laid down next to them. Now two sets of eyes followed Dolby's ball up and down.

"Can we ask you a question? Be honest."

"Sure."

"Have you noticed anything unusual about Steele lately?"

"Oh. One hundred percent." Her answer surprised them.

"Really?"

"Yeah, but remember, I didn't know him much at all before. You guys didn't seem to notice or care, so I just assumed nothing was wrong."

"What kind of stuff have you noticed?" Dolby was beginning to feel bad for missing signs of problems in his friend's life.

"Oh boy. Where do I start?"

Meanwhile, Steele was at the old Dew Drop Inn packing up the rest of his things. He didn't exactly know where he was going. He just knew that he couldn't stay there. Not right now, anyway.

Hope began to make her case. "The first signal to me that something was wrong was how much he seemed to enjoy mistreating animals. Adele told me about how hard he laughed when smashing frogs with a baseball bat. Then I watched him torture that snake with fire."

"That's just Steele though," defended Dolby.

"Maybe so, but that's also how serial killers get started!" argued Hope. "I think he definitely showed signs of taking out his anger on helpless creatures." The other two friends remained unconvinced. "Okay. How about this? When we all first started hanging out over July 4th, didn't you notice that I was camping with my family, Adele was camping with hers, but Steele was there without his family?"

Dolby interjected. "Yeah, but so was I."

"Okay, good point," said Hope. "But what about when you went to the Hideaway in June? Was he with his dad, or was he alone at his campsite?"

"He actually *was* alone," replied Adele. "But his dad was supposed to join him."

"He never did, did he?" remembered Dolby.

"Yeah, but that's typical. His dad isn't always the most reliable. He works a lot." Adele didn't like where this was going.

"Sounds to me like you are making a lot of excuses," Hope observed. "How about . . . where did he go immediately after the Fourth of July trip?"

"He and I went to the treehouse to revisit the crime scene again," said Adele.

"Right. Did you know he spent that night there at the treehouse? He never went home. After spending three days away from his dad, he didn't go right home, which is what we all did."

Dolby considered that for a second. "I hate to admit it, but he has spent the night with me a lot lately—a lot more than usual. And a lot of those times he did invite himself."

"He has also been staying at the treehouse a lot as well," added Adele. "Is he avoiding home for some reason?"

"It was when we were at Gomer Ranch that I began to wonder the most. Did either of you see where he was staying?"

"He said we was hiding out in a cabin in case something happened."

"That may have been partly true," said Hope, "but I went to find him the day we were planning the rescue. I found his cabin, but he wasn't there. I opened the door to find it full of evidence that he had been living there longer than a just a couple of days."

"Really?" they both asked.

"Yeah—he had a clothesline extending the length of the room full of clothes drying. It was way more clothes than he would wear on one weekend. Plus, he had two suitcases full of other clothes. Made me think he had been living there for a while."

"Have you noticed also how late to things he always seems to be these days? If he was coming all the way from the Ranch, that would explain it," continued Adele.

"Now that you mention it, he was unusually quiet at Geema's that day she told us about how animal half-tails share the same characteristics," said Dolby.

"He said he felt sick from eating cherries," added Adele.

"Again, a whole bunch of excuses." Hope wasn't done making her case.

"I did wonder about one other thing," said Adele. "Do you remember when he showed us the silencer at camp? He said he texted a picture to one of his dad's friends who was in the Marines to figure out what it was. His *dad* was in the Marines. Why didn't he just ask his dad first? Oh, and if his dad is the expert when it comes to rehabbing and helping animals recover, why didn't he ask him to help make plans for the . . ." Adele caught herself. She almost blew the surprise. Dolby didn't seem to notice. He was too busy kicking himself for missing the clues that all connected and pointed to problems with Swampy Canis.

"You don't think . . ." Dolby paused. He didn't want to say it, but Adele finished the sentence for him.

". . . that his dad has had a relapse and is drinking again?"

"Did any of you notice how funny he was acting at the vault when we found the article? Maybe he was worried his dad would come home drunk while we were there."

"Remember, too, that Swampy was nowhere to be found all night long at the races. Do you suppose he was visiting the beer stands?"

They all got very quiet again.

"How did we miss all of those signs?" Dolby suddenly didn't think so highly of his detective skills.

43

BLUEPRINTS

"I just wanted to show you cool animals."

—Benjamin Mee in *We Bought a Zoo* (2008)

Adele told him he had no choice—he was going to the haunted mental asylum in Flemings Mill whether he liked it or not. Dolby was already on edge when Farmer Brown picked him up in the familiar Ford F-150 truck. So, it didn't help his anxiety when both Steele and Hope jumped out from under a blanket in the backseat. Dolby hated being surprised. He began to have suspicions about the real plans for the evening when Clayton Brown seemed overly excited about being a chaperone to a Halloween event. "You're gonna love it!" he gushed.

When Adele scolded him with a "Dad! Hush!" he knew for sure something was up. He watched as Mr. Brown turned in a different direction than towards Flemings Mill.

"Um, hello? Where are we going?" Dolby finally asked.

"We are going to see a man about a horse," giggled Hope, trying to keep the secret going.

"Um, Hope, dear? Don't ever use that saying again. It's what people say when they are leaving to use the bathroom!" stated Mr. Brown from the front.

She blushed. "Are you serious? Oh, no. I think I've used that before, too."

Dolby was too preoccupied to laugh. "Guys? Tell me where we are going!"

Steele couldn't resist. "We're going to go drop the kids off at the pool, right Hope?!" His laughter ended quickly. "Oooooof. You punch waaaaay harder than Adele," he said while rubbing his arm.

"You'll see soon where we are going," was all that Adele would divulge. They arrived at Gomer Ranch and parked at the front in the middle of the turnaround. The door was unlocked, and they led Dolby to the back to the camp offices. Uncle Veep was the only one around. He stared down at something spread out on the long, boardroom table. Upon seeing them enter, he swiftly rolled up the scroll and a snapped a rubber band around it. Veep tried to hide it behind his back but it was too late.

Mr. Brown looked at Dolby with anticipation. "You're really gonna love it!" Dolby scanned every face. Each one registered a smile. Uncle Veep handed him the poster. The boy held it like he holds baseball bats—without really knowing what to do. They had to prod him to open it. The second he removed the rubber band and laid it down on the table, many hands helped him unroll it. After paper weights were placed on each corner, Dolby and the rest of them stared. They looked like generals in a war room planning their next move. Maybe it was the pressure of all eyes being on him to see how he would respond, but it wasn't making much sense to him. All he saw was a blur of blue lines, blue dashes, and blue boxes.

Finally, Steele spoke up. "They're blueprints."

Dolby figured that much. "Yeah, but to what?" They had to walk him through it.

"I got the idea after seeing the wounds and injuries from the Campaign of Speckles," said Steele. "I thought about my dad's rehab facility for pit bulls. Made me think we could build a sanctuary for deer—a place to take care of the injured; a place of safety for the weaker ones. We could call it Gomer Deer Preserve or something. The more people I talked to, the bigger the project became. So, this is what we came up with. Here's the main building," Steele traced the outline with his finger. "It could be like an educational center and museum. Schools could bring kids for field trips."

"We thought this could be a petting zoo and a place where children could feed the deer," added Adele. "The barn would have stables for deer that need extra attention. We could see if Red, or Gus, or Monster Horn, or Shadow would be willing to give saddled deer rides to kids in this pen."

Hope wanted to be a part of the discussion. "We thought about deer-themed playgrounds and a merry-go-round with fiberglass deer to ride instead of horses."

"What are these?" Dolby pointed to random rectangles spread throughout the blueprint.

"Those are covered shelters for the rehabbing deer confined to the enclosure."

"Imagine if we had a place like this for deer like Princess or Speckles that suffered an injury or got sick?"

"So, what's all of this—like open pasture?"

Veep jumped in. "That's the best part. It's more than forty acres of protected woods, hills, streams, and lakes for the deer to enjoy. We could even turn it into something like an African safari where visitors could explore them in their natural habitat on golf carts." Every eye glared at him. "Okay. Maybe not golf carts. Something else. We'll figure it out."

Steele anticipated Dolby's next question. "You could communicate to them what was available. I could see a secret entrance for those who need help, or in times when hunting is too high of a threat. Then they could depart after hunting season is over. All you would have to do is let them know what's here for them." Dolby immediately thought of Navi, the dwarf deer, who could live in the sanctuary full-time.

"Deer could come here to have their fawns in safety." Dolby said. "There are so many possibilities. But wait. How *is* this even possible? Who's going to pay for all this?"

"Me and my extended family," blurted Veep proudly. He then got somber. "I figure it's the least we can do for what my brother put you and the deer through. He was the one who kidnapped you. It is his fault that Speckles is dead. It's his fault that other deer were wounded. This is my family's way of making it up to you all. Okay, it would also provide us with a huge tax break. Besides, think about it! A deer park in Gomer? How cool is that?"

"First Turkeytown, and now this? Gomer is going to blow up!" Steele said.

Veep continued. "We would cover the cost of the initial build. Then in the future, it could run on corporate sponsors, private donors, state and federal grants—stuff like that. I have lots of fundraising experience. I would love to network for the park. Besides, I also have lots of rich friends who have money just burning holes in their pockets to give away. What d'ya think Dolby?"

"I'm honestly speechless, except . . " Dolby hesitated.

"Out with it, son!" Veep couldn't imagine any downside to his proposal. "This is a win-win for everyone. What's the problem?"

"It's just. I guess . . . I'm confused, that's all."

"Confused? About what?" Veep now joined Dolby in his confusion.

Dolby measured his words carefully. "It doesn't make sense to me that you would dish out all this money and promise to do all this work for animals that you clearly hate."

"I'm sure I don't know what you are talking about, young man," replied Uncle Veep.

"The Lair. The secret room of your house. You killed all those deer and stuffed them . . . and for what? Peev told us all about how you murdered all those animals." The room grew awkwardly quiet as all eyes now focused on Uncle Veep awaiting an answer.

44

JOURNAL

"God does not stop at rescuing us;
the purpose of that rescue is to enjoy fellowship with us."

—A.W. Tozer

"Ohhh," Veep answered with a knowing nod of the head. "Peev showed you my den, huh? What a great brother I have. Listen to me closely—I didn't kill any of those creatures. No, the only deer that I've ever killed was Princess, and I felt that I had no choice but to do that. I'm still broken up about it."

"Peev said you were the one who hunted down all of those poor deer," challenged Steele further.

"Of course, he said that," responded Veep. "Look—he was using that room to try to convince you that I was the monster behind this plot to destroy Gomer's deer. He was trying to keep you from suspecting him."

"So, if you didn't kill those animals, who did?" asked Adele.

"That's actually a good question—one that I can't completely answer. It all started over twenty years ago when I was driving down one of Gomer's back roads and witnessed a truck hit and kill an eight-point buck, and then drive off. I called a buddy of mine who worked for the Michigan Department of Transportation to ask him what I should do. He said that unless I wanted to take the body for meat, he would just call the hazard recovery company that MDOT contracts out to remove the roadkill. I had no interest in eating the poor thing, but it was a beautiful creature and I just couldn't bring myself to have it thrown away like garbage. That's when I had my first deer head mounted and placed upon my wall at home. I felt like I was giving him dignity and purpose in some weird way. That's how it all started. I asked my friend to alert me when any other deer were killed along Gomer's roads. I asked park rangers to let me know when deer were shot and killed in hunting accidents and never found by the hunter. I made connections with different deer sanctuaries and zoos all over Michigan offering to take off of their hands any deer, elk, moose, gazelles, or caribou that had passed away from illness or old age in order to preserve them. I have been collecting stuffed deer and similar-type species ever since. I found that deer had become dear to me and I enjoyed their beauty so much that it became a hobby of mine to preserve their beauty. I visit that room all the time to admire those graceful creatures. Every animal in my *secret lair*, as Peev calls it, has a unique story that I'm trying to tell."

Hope thought about that for a second, and added, "They would make a great addition to the Deer Preserve Museum, wouldn't they Uncle Veep?"

Veep loved that she was now calling him that, and he loved her suggestion. "I can't think of a better place for them. What d'ya think about all of this now, Dolby?"

The half-tail kept his head down to hide tears of joy. A lone tear splattered on a blue line, causing it to smear. "I think . . . I think it's perfect. I wouldn't change a thing."

Even though Dolby had already shown his mother and grandmother pictures of the blueprints that night, he sat up in bed scrolling and zooming through them as if they were the first time he'd laid eyes on them. He couldn't wait until it was a reality. Of course, he didn't know what role he would play. Deerkeeper? Tour guide? Deer ride coordinator? All three? Something else? He dreamed of the possibilities. He picked up his newest notebook and looked through the first three pages. Instead of three columns dedicated to suspects, reasons for suspicion, and motives, he had three pages dedicated to something else. Under the word *search* Dolby had already filled half of the page with quotes from the Bible and other places—passages like "Seek first the kingdom of God," and "You will seek me and find me, when you seek me with all your heart," and "Search me, O God, and know my heart." Under the word *rescue*, he had listed even more quotes about God's rescue plan. His favorite was from Psalm 18—"He brought me out into a broad place; he rescued me, because he delighted in me." The third page titled *mission* had just one entry so far. It was a quote from *The Kite Runner* that always made him laugh— "It is now your duty to hone that talent, because a person who wastes his God-given talents is a donkey." Dolby knew God was calling him into a new kind of life mission. He was excited to find out what was in store. He had also included one name listed under the word *mission*. Of course, the name was Steele. His friend needed him, and Dolby hadn't been there. He would now be there for him. Dolby wrote down Steele's name because he now knew that part of his mission was to help Steele get through this difficult time. His father was drinking again, and Steele needed his friend's support.

He bowed his head to pray. This time he closed his eyes.

"God undertook the most dramatic rescue operation in cosmic history.
He determined to save the human race from self-destruction, and
He sent His Son Jesus Christ to salvage and redeem them.
The work of man's redemption was accomplished at the cross."
—Billy Graham